mC

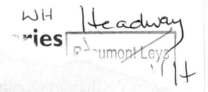

THE MORGAN HORSE

Birch and Asa Tucker owned a fine string of Morgan horses, one of which was Birch's particular favourite. Then the horse turned up in Battleboro without its owner. Birch had been shot and left for dead, and so, with murder in his heart, Asa set out after the bushwhackers. However, he landed up in jail in Barnum, where a lynch mob stood waiting. The scene was set for a bloody war between townsmen and ranchers, and soon lead began to fly . . .

CLINT O'CONNER

THE MORGAN HORSE

Complete and Unabridged

LINFORD
Leicester

First published in Great Britain in 1999 by
Robert Hale Limited
London

First Linford Edition
published 2000
by arrangement with
Robert Hale Limited
London

The moral right of the author has been asserted

British Library CIP Data

O'Conner, Clint
   The Morgan horse.—Large print ed.—
Linford western library
1. Western stories
2. Large type books
I. Title
823.9'14 [F]

ISBN 0–7089–5710–2

Published by
F. A. Thorpe (Publishing)
Anstey, Leicestershire

Set by Words & Graphics Ltd.
Anstey, Leicestershire
Printed and bound in Great Britain by
T. J. International Ltd., Padstow, Cornwall

This book is printed on acid-free paper

1

The People

He was a stocky, handsome, dark bay with a wavy mane, a full tail, a good head and dark, intelligent eyes.

His parents were solid, sturdy animals. His name was Justin Morgan. 'Morgan' was the name of the man who acquired Justin as a youngster in payment for a debt.

Justin Morgan was an 'American' horse. For his height and weight he could out-pull imported European horses of equal size and weight. In stamina and intelligence he proved superior too.

He was foaled in New England in 1748. His descendants were the mounts of choice during the American Revolution. As a stallion he imparted his greatness until the American Morgan

Horse Society was founded. His descendants were indisputably Morgans.

Other breeds mostly imported, would come and go but the American Morgan horse was the choice, not only for work but for endurance. Justin's descendants pulled the prairie schooners during the opening and settling of the American West. They were the saddle animals for herders of great cattle drives.

It was noted that the Morgan horse and frontiersmen not only shared a harrowing existence but the rider and his horse had enough in common to be alike.

After the great trail drives diminished, the herders and their horses went about creating order from Indiandom's chaos.

Birch Tucker, a wild-horse trapper after the era of trail drives ended, and his handsome bay horse Jess put together enough money to homestead the lawful allotment of 160 acres. Jess pulled the logs for the house and barn, for the corrals and fencing. Jess died in his twenty-second year. Birch died two years later. His woman was Lakota, his two sons, Birch Junior and Asa had been following their father's course; they bought out starving homesteaders, expanded the Tucker holdings until shortly before Birch Senior's passing, the Tucker brand — Pothook B T — was on the ribcage of 400 cows, ten up-graded bulls, a sizeable remuda of using horses which showed distinctly the Justin Morgan looks and characteristics.

Asa was the youngest, 28. Birch Junior was the eldest and in many ways the wisest — 32.

Throughout the Low Hill country of southern Colorado and northern New Mexico the Pothook B T mark was known.

The settlement of Battleboro, originally called Hide Town, had grown right along with Birch Tucker and by the time he passed on what had once been a buffalo-hide peddlers' tipi town had flourished until it changed its name and had business establishments on both sides of the wide roadway.

The southern Methodists got a toehold as did Rory Kildare who owned the saloon two doors south of the stage and freight company's corralyard, which was owned and operated by a bull-necked burly man, powerfully disliked, named Sam Brown, who also disliked Indians. He had what he considered good reason, his parents and brother had been massacred in Texas years back by Comanches.

What kept Battleboro's merchants from doing more business than they did was the lack of a railroad siding east of town.

Some day it would come, but by the time it did Battleboro would have become a city instead of a town.

Most folks favoured the railroad. Cowmen particularly liked the idea of shipping cattle rather than driving them a hundred miles westerly to the nearest town with a siding and holding corrals. But that's how it had been done since Birch Tucker's day. It was a tradition; the sell-off of local cattle were gathered, driven to the outskirts of Battleboro and when all the herds were junctured, local stockmen would join in the six-day drive to Barnum where the railroad had a siding, corrals and loading chutes.

Because old Birch was one of the earliest cattlemen in the Low Hill country, late-coming cattlemen accepted his leadership, which was understandable. Asa was young and wild. His brother was older, showed more Indian blood and was more thoughtful, taciturn and individualistic.

The other cattlemen knew the Tucker 'boys'. They had accompanied their father on every drive for ten years. There were four other big outfits, three were owned by older men. Whether their scepticism was justified or not, they were older and for that reason in particular did not take kindly to old Birch's lads assuming their pa's hard-won respect and leadership.

When the older cowmen congregated

in Kildare's saloon they found a kindred spirit. Rory Kildare, a large and powerful man as well as being a willing brawler, made no secret of his dislike of 'them' breed In'ian Tuckers'.

What might have passed as silent disapproval became something else when Asa Tucker courted the corralyard owner's pretty daughter, a girl of sixteen with blue eyes and blonde hair named Betsy Brown.

Birch Junior favoured the Lakota. Asa favoured his pa, he was dark-eyed but light skinned. In other ways the brothers were different, but they had inherited their father's conviction that blood mattered, not eye colour, nor hide colour, but kinship. Kinship mattered.

It was tedious work spread over weeks of saddlebacking, missing meals and hunkering around small fires on cold nights because it was too far to ride home.

Separating, making a gate count

required several days. When the sell-off was ready there was more saddlebacking; it was customary to keep the gather close and cattle tended to drift when graze got short.

Every year it was the same and had been for many years. Six, seven hundred pound cattle whose mammy cows had gone dry so long ago there hadn't been any association between cows and February calves for seven or eight months. But the bawling was the same; confined cattle just naturally bellowed their complaint.

The Tuckers kept three seasonal riders. Each man had come north to work for Pothook B T for several years. They were good men, hardened, knowledgeable stockmen.

One of them named Alamo Taunton, a gangling redheaded Texan with a notable Adam's apple, teased Asa about the corralyard man's daughter. Alamo Taunton was a natural tease but he was likeable, good-natured, generous and plenty savvy.

Asa had been teased for years by the redheaded Texan. In time he developed a knack for teasing back, which amused the other men.

But teasing Asa about his budding romance was different. For one, Betsy's father, a high-strung and opinionated individual hadn't noticed Asa's visits until Rory Kildare mentioned it, then he had a fit. He was a widower with one child. Betsy was the apple of his eye and, as she had budded out, her father had developed a protectiveness that was stifling. He ran off town boys with profanity and threats.

When there was talking of incorporating the Low Hill country into a county of Colorado, Betsy's father told the town marshal, who would become sheriff if the incorporation succeeded, that the next time he caught that Tucker boy around his daughter he was going to horsewhip him, and the marshal, a bull of a greying individual with an easy-going disposition told the corralyard boss talk like that could get him not

8

only hurt, but jailed until the cows came home.

For Asa Tucker during gathering time, the days began before dawn and ended with dead tired men and horses after sundown. There was no time to ride to town.

Folks stopped calling the old man's son Junior a year or two after the first Birch Tucker died, which suited the eldest son fine, he had never liked being called 'Junior'.

Like Asa and the hired hands, Birch was in the saddle when it was cold and stayed there until dying days cooled off.

He never visited Battleboro except out of necessity so he had no idea his brother was 'fancying' the corralyard man's daughter.

It's doubtful if he had known he would have said anything. Like his father, he minded Pothook B T. It had always been his life and would continue to be as long as he lived. Also, he shunned small-town gossip.

As he had once told his mother several years before she died, looking more Indian than white was a cross he'd had to bear not only as a schoolboy but in later social contacts. When she had said she was sorry, young Birch had replied bluntly, 'I'm not ashamed of you. I'm proud to be your son.'

But Birch was not blind to minor slights; he had endured them in school so in later life when he was owner of one of the largest ranches for a thousand miles and people were more subtle, he let it roll off him like water off a duck's back. Rory Kildare had one of those large pictures of the 1876 Custer battle framed and prominently displayed above his back bar.

Once, when he had been drinking and Birch Tucker was washing dust from his throat, the barman had said, 'We got even for what them tomahawks done to Gen'ral Custer,' and Birch finished his beer, put a coin beside the glass, looked steadily at the barman and had said, 'Who are *we*, Rory? You wasn't there,' and the saloonman shot back, 'I didn't have to be there. It's always been us against them.'

Birch's father would have jumped over the bar; Birch's temperament was different. He ordered another jolt and threw it in the face of Rory Kildare, left the saloon and did not go back.

A Texas cowman named Bruce Evans who had been at the bar spoke while watching Rory wiping off with his bar towel.

'You're lucky he didn't break your nose.'

An old man down the bar a few feet said, 'Birch an' his boys is hard workers and honest. Don't make any difference who their ma was.' The old man put coins on the bar and departed.

As with most slights when it was not kept alive people lost interest. When the local gossip got stale there was always the weather.

It rained for five days straight, which made gathering cattle frustrating and uncomfortable, but Birch and his brother set examples.

Their riders suffered without comment; the gather had to be made regardless of the weather. The existence of rangemen had never been a bed of roses and never would be.

On the day when the rain stopped, the sun came out and the world steamed, they finished the gather. For the next four days they made the gate-cut, animals to be sold and animals, mostly cows or young animals, were choused away.

The sell-down cattle were either intuitively or just naturally restless and since there was no corral in the land large enough to hold hundreds of cattle, the Pothook B T men took turns riding nighthawk and daytime holding them together. A lot of cattle in one place ate a lot of graze and browse.

Birch sent his brother to see if the other cow outfits were ready for the annual converging over by Battleboro.

To reach the Evans Ox Shoe outfit, Asa rode easterly and when he was passing to the north of town he yielded to temptation.

He hadn't been able to see the corralyard boss's daughter in weeks. He visited the tonsorial parlour to get shaved, shorn and liberally sprinkled with French toilet water, had a meal at the only eatery in Battleboro, went up to sit on the bench outside Kildare's saloon, which was opposite the corralyard and watch for Betsy, who kept books for her father.

It was afterwards noted that this was his first mistake. His second mistake was to become restless with waiting and to cross the road to the bench outside the corralyard office next to the roadway door and the only window in the office.

Betsy saw him, left her table and went out front. She glowed and Asa patted the bench where she sat down as she said, 'Are you gathering?'

'Just finished,' he told her. 'I thought of you every day.'

Her colour heightened; she avoided

looking at him. 'I thought that was it, the other ranchers are gathering . . . Asa?'

'Yes.'

'Nothing. I was going to say I sure missed you.'

He felt for her hand and held it. 'We'll be back in a few weeks. In time for the grange's party an' dancin'.'

She still avoided eye contact. 'Maybe something'll come up, Asa.'

He replied and squeezed her hand at the same time. 'Nothing'll keep me from that . . . Betsy?'

'If I can, Asa. Pa has ideas about that, and other things.'

Before young Tucker could respond, Betsy's father flung out of the office door and pointed a rigid finger at Asa. 'You let go her hand! Don't let me ever catch you near her again, or I'll horsewhip you within an inch of your life. *Get away from her*!'

Asa gave a final squeeze arose and made his third mistake, instead of looking elsewhere he stood facing

Betsy's father. That was too much for the irascible and agitated older man. He took one step closer and fired a cocked fist.

Asa went down and stayed down. His hat landed in the manured roadway. Betsy sprang up, would have gone to young Tucker, but her father caught her by the arm, hurled her through the open door and slammed it.

There were spectators on both sides of the road, but there were more of them on the plankwalk in front of the saloon.

A lanky rangeman named Bob Whitney crossed from the saloon side, ignored Betsy's father and helped young Asa back on to the bench. Asa had a torn lip, blood on the front of his shirt and when the rangeman retrieved his hat and dropped it where it belonged, Betsy's father abruptly entered his office and slammed the door.

Bob Whitney's example sparked other men to arrive. One of them handed Asa a pony and told him to drink, which Asa did, and afterwards had a coughing fit. He was not accustomed to whiskey but it served its purpose.

He felt his swelling mouth, reset his hat, looked at the other men and got unsteadily to his feet. The rangeman named Bob Whitney stepped between Asa and the office's roadway door. Most of the little crowd drifted away. The saloon across the road was the ideal place to discuss what had happened.

Asa's face was swelling but very little blood trickled from his mouth. With deliberate slowness he pulled loose the tie-down thong over his holstered sidearm.

Bob Whitney shook his head. He was a few years older than Asa, knew Birch better than Asa, and rode for Ox Shoe. He quietly said, 'Don't do it, Asa. You shoot that cranky son of a bitch an' his girl'll never forget it.'

Whitney also said, 'Go home; leave it be, for a while anyway.'

'I was on my way to see Bruce Evans. We've finished gatherin'.'

Whitney jerked his head. 'Get your horse an' we'll ride out yonder together.'

Asa's horse was at the livery barn. By the time he'd got down there and got saddled up, Bob Whitney appeared in the roadway out front.

The liveryman hadn't seen what had happened and he was too savvy to ask about the bloody shirt and purple swelling. Curiosity got an awful lot of cats hurt.

They had to ride nearly the full length of Battleboro. People on both sides of the road watched in silence. Asa and his companion ignored them.

Bob Whitney had no outstanding characteristics. He looked like dozens of seasonal rangemen. He was average in height, maybe in his thirties and everything he owned from his boots to his hat was worn and scuffed. He had one attribute: he was a top hand.

If he had another appreciable characteristic it was fearlessness. He was a good hand, a good worker and a fair poker player. Those were the things folks knew about him and they were enough.

By the time they had Ox Shoe's buildings in sight, Whitney had told Asa Tucker they were getting close to completing their gather.

Asa had reason to listen without replying except to tell his companion that was what he had intended to ride out to Ox Shoe to determine.

2

A Crisis

Bruce Evans had been helped to get established more than twenty years earlier by old Birch Tucker. When the annual drive was ready and there was grumbling, he very outspokenly said Birch Tucker's eldest son was leader as far as he was concerned.

Evans was a weathered man, a widower who worked hard for long hours to eventually build up a cow outfit worthy of anyone's respect. Except for Birch Junior and Asa, Bruce Evans was the only other person asked to help with the old man's coffin and burial. Until his sons were old enough, Bruce Evans had been a son to old Birch.

When Bob Whitney and Asa stopped in front of the Evans barn to dismount and tie up, Bruce Evans came through from the corrals out back and stopped stone-still in the wide front barn opening.

Bob Whitney said, 'There wasn't no mail, Bruce.'

Evans seemed not to have heard. 'What in hell happened to *him*?'

Whitney looked at Asa for the explanation. Asa said, 'I got hit. It don't amount to much. Birch wants to know if you're ready to meet for the drive.'

Evans walked closer and addressed his rider. 'What happened, Bob?'

Whitney weaselled. 'Asa'll tell you.'

Asa changed the subject. 'If you're ready we'll meet you outside of town like always.'

Bruce Evans shook his head. 'Asa . . . ?'

'It don't matter. I'll take care of it. What'll I tell Birch?'

'Two more days an' we'll make the drive to town. Asa . . . ?'

'I'll tell Birch. I'd better get home or I'll miss supper.'

Evans and his top hand did not say another word as they watched Asa mount, turn and ride out of the yard. When he was a fair distance off, Bob Whitney said, 'Sam Brown knocked him senseless for talkin' to his daughter.'

'Just talkin'?'

' 'Far as I know. They was sittin' on the bench outside the office. I guess he saw 'em through the window. He come out yellin', knocked Asa down shoved Betsy inside and slammed the door. Me'n some fellers did what we could do. That's about it.'

Evans put a steady glare on Whitney. 'I don't think so, Bob. When he gets home lookin' like he's been drug through a meat grinder, Birch'll go huntin' for Sam.'

Whitney shrugged. 'Nothin' we can do, Bruce.'

Evans went back into the barn where he'd been forking feed to the using horses and for a long time after finishing he leaned on the three-tined hay fork.

He knew Birch like a brother. Birch was one of those men who didn't act rashly but when something like this happened he would know why, and that was something Birch Tucker had tolerated most of his life. But his brother coming home bloodied . . .

Bruce Evans had one other rider besides Bob Whitney, a rock-built man of few words named Werner Copland. When they were having supper Bruce Evans asked Bob Whitney if Bob had mentioned the trouble in town to Werner. When Bob nodded, Bruce told them both he was going over to Pothook B T in the morning; they could bring in the last few stragglers for the drive. He thought he'd be back before sundown.

Whitney and Copland accepted this without interrupting their meal. Three riders were better than two but there wasn't all that much left to do.

Bruce was gone before Bob and Werner rolled out. Neither of them was surprised.

It was a fair ride from Ox Shoe to Pothook B T. If a man didn't push his horse and providing he left in the wee hours he would arrive in the Tucker yard about sun-up. It was open country most of the way and it was also dark.

When Bruce Evans reached the yard the hired hands were at breakfast. He tied up, did not heed the dark main house but went to the bunkhouse. When he walked in, the eating men stonily looked up. One of them told him to join them at breakfast.

Bruce Evans said, 'Thanks. Where's Birch?'

Alamo Taunton said, 'Asa's at the house. Birch is gone.'

'Gone?'

'His horse an' outfit was gone at the barn.' Taunton twisted on his bench to look at Bruce Evans. 'Somethin' wrong?'

Bruce went closer, filled a cup with black coffee before answering. 'Did he ride to town?' he asked.

The rangemen did not know when or

where their employer had gone. Alamo Taunton persisted, 'What is it?'

'You saw Asa?'

'We saw him. He got into a fight in town. Nothin' unusual about that.' The other rangeman, Walter Corrigan, agreed.

'Sam Brown knocked him senseless for talkin' to Sam's daughter.'

The seated men did not say a word but Bruce Evans did, 'Birch more'n likely went to hunt Sam up.'

The riders wouldn't question that. Birch and his brother were close as peas in a pod. Taunton also drew off a cup of coffee, his second and with one booted foot on the bench where he had been sitting considered Bruce Evans. 'Maybe he won't find him,' he said in a voice lacking conviction.

'He'll find him. I figured he wouldn't be gone yet.' Bruce put the cup down. 'You boys finished gatherin'?'

Taunton replied. 'We're finished. You?'

'Pretty near. We'll meet you over at

24

the holding ground outside Battleboro. If you see Birch before I do . . . tell him that.'

On the ride back the way he had come Bruce Evans had an unpleasant thought. He and Birch could have passed in the dark, him going west, Birch going east.

He was satisfied that by the time he reached town it would be over.

By the time he had rooftops in sight smoke was rising from breakfast fires. As he was leaving his animal to be cared for, the liveryman said, 'You're up an' stirrin' early.'

Evans's reply ignored that. He asked if Birch Tucker had ridden in.

'Not here he ain't. Is he supposed to? You gents ready to make the drive?'

Bruce walked out into the roadway. Things seemed normal, if there'd been trouble things would be different. He went over to the eatery where the caféman was feeding hungry and impatient townsmen.

Bruce nodded to the town marshal

who nodded back as he used the identical words the liveryman had used and Bruce sat down beside him, shook his head at the caféman and asked the town marshal if he'd seen Birch Tucker.

The larger man shook his head until he'd swallowed then spoke. 'Not for a week or more. Why? You ready to start the drive?'

Bruce said he was ready, and left the café.

An early rising sun had little warmth but it brought good light and visibility.

Bruce stood outside the eatery. Birch wouldn't be at the saloon but could be at the corralyard. Bruce crossed over, walked up there and got an enormous sense of relief. Sam Brown was supervising his two yardmen as they backed a pair of 1,200-pound horses on to the pole. The morning southbound was scheduled to leave Battleboro on time and if folks could say one favourable thing about Sam Brown it was that his rigs kept to schedule, barring accidents.

The corralyard man did not notice Evans; between seeing to the hitch and boarding passengers he was too occupied, so the cowman strolled toward the north-west corner of the yard to look at corralled livestock, the most natural thing in the world to do for stockmen.

Brown cared for his animals well, there was not a rib showing even among the mules, big, stout jennys. There were close to fifteen animals who had recently been fed and were now willing to stand perfectly still waiting for the sun to warm them.

One large chestnut was facing west, eyes half closed, absorbing new-day warmth. Bruce hesitated before turning back; there was something about the chestnut. It was standing beside a mule. Evans moved along the peeled stringers until he could see the chestnut better and stopped stone still. The horse was marked on the left shoulder with one of those small irons used on horses as opposed to the larger branding irons used on cattle.

The brand was a smaller version of Pothook B T.

Bruce climbed between stringers, worked his way closer to re-examine the mark, then studied the horse. If it had been ridden there should have been marks of the saddle blanket.

The horse had chaff in its mane and tail. It had rolled; there was no blanket stain.

He climbed out of the corral about the time Sam Brown waved for the driver to leave the yard. Brown was still standing there looking roadward when Bruce tapped his shoulder. The corralyard man turned.

Evans had one question. 'Where'd you get that chestnut in the corral, Sam?'

Brown answered without hesitation. 'Bought him off a couple of travellin' horse traders.'

'Did you see his brand?'

Brown nodded. 'Couldn't help but

see it. They give me a bill of sale. It's a Pothook B T animal.' Brown studied the cowman a moment before also saying, 'You want to buy him?'

'No. I want to see the feller who rode him.'

'They wasn't ridin' him, they was leadin' him.'

'Didn't you recognize him? That's Birch's special animal.'

Brown shifted weight. He did not like standing for any length of time. 'Bruce, horses are traded every day. He looked familiar; the Tuckers sold horses over the years with their mark on 'em. They're all around.'

'But not that horse, Sam.'

'What are you gettin' at?' the corralyard man said, sounding irritable.

'I'm lookin' for Birch.'

'He'd be at the ranch.'

'I just came from there. He left before sun-up. Who are the traders you bought his horse from?'

Brown's annoyance was increasing. He was just naturally an irritable individual. 'They come in every few days to peddle me horses. Mostly, I never saw 'em before. I look for bowed tendons, contracted hooves, kidney sores and cold mouths, I don't pay much heed to the peddlers. They ask a price, I make an offer and in nine cases out of ten I get the animal.'

'You haven't seen Birch?'

'No! Why should I? We got nothin' in common except his brother tryin' to spark my daughter.'

'An' you hit him.'

'Yes, I hit him. When my girl marries it won't be to no damned 'breed no matter what he's worth.' Brown paused, pinched his eyes narrow and said, 'That's why you're lookin' for Birch? Because you figure In'ian-like he'll come lookin' for me for runnin' off his brother? He can come when he's ready. Now I got work to do.'

Bruce reached to detain Brown. 'Who sold you his horse?'

'I already told you, I got no idea. I didn't ask names.'

'What'd they look like?'

'Like all them raggedy-assed, ridin'-through-traders look. Hadn't shaved, was dirty. The one with sorrel hair was maybe forty. The other one hardly said a word. He was a skinny feller with some missin' teeth. Bruce, I got work to do.'

For Evans the search of town for two strangers answering the description Brown had supplied was wasted time until he visited Hornsby's General Store.

The aged watery-eyed clerk remembered a man with sorrel hair and his companion shy teeth in front. They had bought the kind of supplies travellers acquire. The clerk remembered little except that the man shy front teeth didn't say a word, he left that to the burly, older man with sorrel hair.

The clerk verified that the pair had filled army-style saddle-bags and had left Battleboro travelling on the south-east stage road an hour or such a matter after the store opened for business, which would be about seven o'clock.

Bruce went down to the livery barn for his horse and pondered. The strangers didn't have that much lead, especially if they weren't hurrying. He was well mounted, could possibly overtake the strangers long before they got in the vicinity of Barnum.

Whether he caught them or not it would be a long ride and the other stockmen would be driving to the juncture west of town. They wouldn't wait.

He led his horse out to be saddled and although the affable liveryman wanted to chatter, Bruce Evans responded to nothing the liveryman said so he gave up.

Bruce led his horse out front to be mounted and had his attention caught by Rory Kildare yelling something while shedding his barman's apron and running across to the corralyard.

Bruce swung across leather and was evening up his reins when Rory Kildare appeared in the corralyard's wide gateway yelling to Evans and flapping his arms.

A ten-minute diversion wouldn't put him too far behind the travelling horse traders so he reined northward.

By the time he reached the wooden gateway there were about a dozen men inside milling around the morning southbound coach which had just arrived.

Brown saw Bruce and gestured. Bruce rode into the yard as the crowd parted enough for several men to drag something out.

Bruce swung off, edged close and stopped breathing for seconds. Birch Tucker was on the ground, bloody and motionless. Sam Brown told three men to carry Birch into his office.

Bruce handed his reins to a dark yardman and followed.

A stocky, short man with a full beard and stagedriver's smoke-tanned gauntlets, the badge of his profession, addressed Sam Brown ignoring everyone else.

'He was lyin' in the road about two miles up country where one of them cattle trails come down to the road.' The whip paused to remove his gloves and fold them under his belt. 'Been shot. Me'n a passenger got him inside . . . Is he dead?'

Bruce shouldered through and knelt. There was blood, Birch's shirt was soaked with it. Finding the wound was difficult. From the appearance it was reasonable to assume it had been a body shot.

It hadn't. Blood running from above came from a hair-matted gouge as wide as a man's finger up alongside the head.

Bruce looked at Rory Kildare and nodded. The saloonman went across the road with a wide stride, got a bottle and returned with it.

Bruce used whiskey to clear the hair, dirt and torn flesh away from the injury, pushed hair aside and leaned down. One of the bystanders said, 'Real gentle-like feel the bone. If it gives to the touch his skull's broke.'

Sam Brown knelt across from Bruce and when the cowman hesitated, Brown leaned far over and with a surprisingly gentle touch followed the bystander's direction.

He leaned back to wipe his hand, looked at Bruce and shook his head. 'Feel for yourself. Skull's not busted.'

With three men on each side of an old horse blanket Birch Tucker was carried to the jailhouse, the only place folks would want to bed down someone dirty and leaking blood.

Bruce told the blacksmith, who was put together like a bear and who served as town marshal in his spare time he would get word to Asa about his brother.

Sam Brown who had helped carry Birch to the jailhouse said he'd send one of his yardmen which would save Bruce Evans from having to ride so far and back.

Bruce was agreeable. He had really spent more time away from his gather than he should have.

After Bruce left, the townsmen sent for a widow-woman to wash Birch. There was no doctor closer than Lexington, a full fledged town southeast eighty miles. The men went up to the saloon to discuss that and other things. For one thing Birch's six-gun had its tie-down in place when he'd been shot. For another thing, who had shot him and why.

He remained unconscious until about sun-up the following morning. He didn't want to talk, his eyes watered and he had a headache that wouldn't quit.

It was late afternoon before Asa and Alamo Taunton arrived. Asa was shocked at his brother's appearance. Alamo Taunton, satisfied Birch wasn't dead, wanted to know who had shot him and that was something no one could say because they did not know.

Sam Brown didn't visit the jailhouse until the third day, by which time Birch had sat up, eaten and talked. He had no idea who had shot him nor why.

He'd used the old cow trail to reach the stage road and was turning south and that was all he remembered. He had seen no one, except for a pair of raffish rangemen, hadn't heard a gunshot and with the headache abating, his head wrapped in a bandage like a Turk's headgear, except for an occasional jolt of whiskey with its temporary buoying effect, he felt like hell. He told the blacksmith-town marshal he felt as bad as he looked and the blacksmith dryly said that would have to be real bad.

Asa brought food from the eatery. Birch ate everything right down to the china. Asa asked the identical set of questions others had asked and got the same answers. One minute Birch was reining southward on to the road and the next he knew he was in a jailhouse cage feeling like ten barefoot men had stomped him and that one had wiped his feet.

He was anxious about the gather. Alamo told him they'd bring the cattle to the holding ground within two

37

days, then he, Walter and Asa would make the drive down to Barnum. He reassured Birch; it would be a big drive and there would be plenty of riders.

On the fourth day with the sound of lowing cattle from different directions making enough noise to require folks in town to yell to be heard, Bruce Evans took Asa and Alamo Taunton aside to tell them where Birch's chestnut was along with how it had got there. He also told them for a damned fact too much time had passed to chase down the men who had sold the chestnut to Sam Brown but he was satisfied they'd ridden in the direction of Barnum.

He ended up saying it would be another three days before they got the drive to Barnum which would mean those two horse traders would have been to Barnum and as far beyond as horsemen could be.

Asa wanted to leave the drive, hasten to Barnum, and Bruce shook his head. Too much time had passed he told the younger man, and added something.

'Barnum isn't so big folks wouldn't remember a feller with missin' front teeth and a sorrel-headed man. If they recollect we can maybe pick up the trail.'

Alamo Taunton agreed but Asa didn't. He wanted those likely shooters of his brother badly enough to abandon the drive to find them.

Reasoning with Asa Tucker when his mind was set was no different than peeing in a creek with the expectation of raising the water level.

Alamo winked at Bruce as he said, 'You'd ought to talk to Birch, Asa.'

It was good advice but since folks could not see into the future it could prove to be something else.

In any case, Asa visited Birch in his jailhouse cage and Birch would not give his approval, not because he feared for his brother's welfare, because with Asa gone that would leave only Alamo and Walter to make the drive, not only from the home place, but on the longer drive. Ordinarily there were four Pothook B T riders.

Asa protested until Birch held up a hand as he said, 'If he was aimin' at my face it was a poor shot. Asa, I'm doin' fine. In a week or so I'll be back in the saddle. Then we can hunt those gents down.'

No one could fault what Birch had said, except his brother. He told Alamo and Walter Corrigan they'd have to make the drive without him. Both men nodded; it would be difficult but they could do it. On the ride back from town, Alamo said, 'Someday he's goin' to get himself killed.'

The husky man riding stirrup with Alamo agreed. 'He's been quick to do things since I've known him. When Birch finds out he'll raise hell an' prop it up.'

Alamo wryly smiled at his companion. 'Birch never throwed a fit in his life. He just ups an' does things without a lot of talk.'

'Yeah. In'ian-like.'

When they got home the gather had

scattered which was understandable, they'd fed off all the holding ground feed. No one swore, they simply spent this day and the day following regathering which was not difficult, just tiresome.

3

The Drive

There were in the neighbourhood of 6-800 cattle at the holding ground. Alamo and Walter brought in the last herd and Bruce Evans lent a hand. When the entire herd was bunched for the drive, the point rider, who had in former years been old Birch Tucker or his eldest son, where there was no Tucker to ride point, a grizzled, disagreeable, older cowman named Bentley Clavenger assumed leadership.

No one protested; the idea was to start the damned drive not argue. In the drag, Bruce Evans drifted back to ride with Corrigan and Taunton. He asked where Asa was and for an answer got two expressionless looks. He swore and rode back on a wing position.

Alamo told Walter the idea was to drive the gawddamned cattle, the feuding could wait, and Walter who was never talkative, nodded his head.

The first day went smoothly. There were something like eleven riders and because the cattle were not pushed but were allowed to snatch feed as they went along, except for an occasional cut-back things went very well. Also, because the ground was still damp there was no dust to irritate the hell out of the Clavenger rider who had been delegated to drive the wagon full of bedrolls and food.

The first night they camped in the same place they'd set up camp for years. Wood was shy but grass and water were plentiful and the objective of cattle drives was not comfort for riders, it was to provide necessities to everlasting hungry critters who had two stomachs and spent their lives trying to keep the first one full.

Some of the riders were seasonal men, mostly they knew each other and

Bob Whitney played his mouth organ after supper to the accompaniment of a Jew's harp played by a Clavenger rangeman.

Bentley Clavenger looked up at the Pothook B T riders and asked about Asa. All Alamo and Walter could tell him was that Asa wasn't with the drive and the old cowman growled and stormed in a characteristic manner and stamped away to tell Bruce Evans those damned Tuckers were an unreliable lot. He should have known better. He said it anyway and Bruce laced him up one side and down the other.

'What'd you expect? Birch is flat down an' his brother's doin' what you'd do, he's huntin' the bushwhacking bastard.'

Clavenger put a sulphurous gaze on Bruce. 'The drive comes first. There's only two Pothook B T riders, the other men got to do more work.'

A lanky, skinny rangeman came up to tell Bent Clavenger his horse was limping and the old man jumped to a characteristic conclusion. 'Some son of a bitch's horse kicked him.'

As the skinny man was leading the way he said, 'No. Your horse rolled and went over an old coyote or wolf trap that'd been in the tall grass lord knows how long. It took four of us to hold him down long enough to spring the old trap loose.'

'How's his back?'

It was not possible to make a cattle drive for any length of time and not encounter difficulties. Old Bentley Clavenger knew that as well as anyone. He briefly looked at his mount's back, told the skinny rangeman to doctor it and went behind the wagon to the rope corral to make sure that the other horse he'd fetched along and had just bought in town was rideable. He was. In fact no one had been on his back for a week and better, but he was a muscled-up, short-back animal with a good eye and lots of mane and tail hair. He was a chestnut. Clavenger had given $27 for him. Ignored the shoulder brand and still ignored it, most likely because it was dark, but he had to have seen it. That's why horses were branded on the left shoulder. They were historically mounted on the left side.

He was riding point on the second day, chewing jerky and wearing an expression folks usually saw on someone who'd been eating raw quinces or rhubarb.

The second day they made excellent time, in fact Bruce Evans told Clavenger if they could keep it up they'd reach Barnum tomorrow. Bruce might have said more but he didn't. He was looking at Clavenger's mount. The old man said, 'Gave twenty-seven dollars for him.'

Bruce ignored that. 'You know whose horse that is?'

'Do I know? I just told you I give sound money for him to — '

'I know who you got him from. That's Birch Tucker's horse.' Bruce pointed to the left shoulder.

Clavenger ignored the pointing arm. 'I got a bill of sale. I saw the brand.

46

I paid good money an' got a bill of sale. No matter who he belonged to, he's mine.'

Bruce was called away by one of the rangemen, they had a big steer with a bad limp. It was an Ox Shoe critter.

The rider said, 'Stepped on somethin'. I thought it was his shoulder or maybe a snake bite. Watch how he goes.'

The injury wasn't as important as what had to be done; a limping steer would not make it all the way to the shipping pens.

The rider said, 'Shoot him?'

Bruce watched the animal as he replied, 'Let him go as long as he can, when he can't go no further . . . '

When they made the second camp at another place they'd made other camps and had the supper fire going, Bruce Evans approached Bentley Clavenger with an offer of twenty-seven dollars for the Pothook B T branded horse and Clavenger's reply was accompanied with a scowl.

'My other horse got his back tore in

the grass by an old wolf trap. What'd I ride if I sold you that horse?'

'There's others, Bent.'

'Not in my outfit. We each brought two horses. I dassn't risk settin' one of my lads afoot . . . Bruce, you got horses, why'n hell you tryin' to beat me out of this one?'

'Because he's Birch's favourite animal.'

'He . . . I got a damned bill of sale, Bruce. He's nobody's horse but mine.'

The older man marched off in the direction of the fire. Bruce returned to his camp. This night he did not sleep well.

In the morning there was a gloomy overcast. When the drive was resumed, Alamo Taunton told Bruce Evans his lame steer had been snake bitten. They let the animal drift off by himself. If it was a rattler that bit him he'd be sick for a couple of weeks, he'd shrink because he wouldn't want to eat.

It began to drizzle, the riders went to the wagon for their ponchos. Clavenger sent a rider ahead because the drizzle hindered visibility and he wanted to know if they would make the shipping pens before nightfall.

The ground hadn't fully recovered from that earlier downpour so 800 cattle were unable to make good time. After the drizzle turned to rain, the rider returned to report that the shipping pens were full of cattle from an easterly drive.

With no longer a need for haste they made camp under a leaden sky, got a fire going, ate and drank coffee.

They were no more than six or eight miles from Barnum. The ranchers conferred. It was decided to stay where they were until the shipping pens had been emptied. The feed was better than it would be closer to Barnum.

Bruce was restless. He waited until it was bedding-down time then saddled up and headed for Barnum. He had no idea what to expect but he would have bet a pocketful of new money Asa was either over there or had been.

Barnum was a bustling community. Wherever the railroad passed, close towns flourished. When he left his horse at the livery barn, the sound of music blended with more lamplight than Battleboro ever had after nightfall.

He knew the town well enough. It had three eateries, four saloons and gaming parlours and two churches, one Southern Baptist the other Methodist.

In Battleboro, folks rarely wasted money on paint. In Barnum almost every building was painted. He had acquaintances in Barnum. One was a beefy deputy sheriff named Bud Lange.

Bud wasn't at the jailhouse so Bruce prowled to find him. Where they met was at a saloon with more lights than a Christmas tree and tobacco smoke almost thick enough to cut with a knife. A balding man with elegant sleeve garters was playing a piano and sweating.

Beside the piano was Bud Lange holding a sudsy glass of beer. When he looked up, saw Bruce on the far edge of the crowd, he put his glass atop the piano and worked his way through people. Where they met near the door the hefty deputy shoved out a hand without smiling and jerked his head. Bruce followed him out into the night where there was less commotion and noise. Lange turned and said, 'Are you alone?'

Bruce shook his head. 'I'm with the annual drive. We're camped some miles west. When'll the pens be empty?'

'Train's due tomorrow, Bruce; when was the last time you saw young Tucker?'

'Four, five days ago. Why?'

'Well, I got him locked up. Sheriff's down south visitin' his daughter an' won't be back maybe for a — '

'You got Asa in jail? What for?'

'He called a redheaded feller out an' shot him.'

'Dead?'

Bud Lange nodded. 'The redheaded

feller was fallin' down drunk. He didn't even know he'd been called.'

Bruce looked for something to sit on, found nothing and gazed at the massively large man with the badge on his vest. 'There was two of 'em, Bud, the redheaded one an' another one with some missin' teeth in front.'

Lange acknowledged a slap on the shoulder given him by a departing saloon customer and responded with a smile.

'Bruce, there wasn't another feller. Why'd young Tucker do somethin' like that?'

'Because the redheaded one and his partner with the missin' teeth shot Birch, stole his horse an' sold it in town, then rode on.'

'Kill Birch?'

'No, but sure put him down for a spell. Bud, what did Asa tell you?'

'Not a damned word except for sayin' it was a fair fight. He called the other feller, they went out into the roadway . . . Bruce, that redheaded feller was so drunk he couldn't find his butt usin' both hands.'

'Can I see him?'

'Sure. You'n him close?'

'His pa was like a father to me. I knew both the boys from knee-high on up. They was family to me.'

The beefy lawman led off on an angling course to the jailhouse where an overhead lamp was turned up high. He pointed to a chair. 'I'll fetch him. Bruce, put your gun on the desk.'

Evidently Asa was asleep. He grumbled, stopped grumbling and said, 'He's here?'

'In the office. We'll change that bandage in the morning. Walk ahead of me.'

In a less bright light Asa wouldn't have looked so bad. His face was swollen and discoloured. One ear was puffed half its normal size.

Bruce said, 'Why didn't you wait? The whole drivin' crew is a few miles east of town.'

Bud Lange dragged a chair around,

put a massive arm on Asa's shoulder as he said, 'Set.'

He then went behind the more cluttered of two desks and built and lighted a smoke.

Asa sat, considered raw knuckles and spoke without looking up. 'When I found 'em they'd trailed some cattle they'd picked up on the way. I think they figured to drive 'em further where the marks wouldn't be familiar.'

Deputy Lange interrupted. 'Bold as brass, Bruce, and ten times as thick. Them cattle was marked with a local brand. They couldn't have sold them in this county for two bits a head. They kept 'em up in a blind canyon. I suspect they figured to spend a little time here then drive their rustled beef further along.' Lange killed his cigarette. 'They don't come any stupider, but the cattle was drove back where they belonged an' that ain't the problem anyway. Young Tucker murdered that redheaded feller in plain sight. Half the town saw him do it. When the sheriff gets back he — '

Bruce interrupted. 'Asa, for Chris'-sake . . . '

'It was a fair fight. I told him who I was, brother to the feller he shot and stole his horse. I called him, an' he went outside with me.'

Bud Lange had to interrupt again, 'Asa, that man . . . I don't think he understood a damned word you said. Every one in the saloon would have bet he'd pass out before he reached the road. Bruce?'

'What?'

'He stood out there saggin' from side to side. He didn't know which side his holster was on. He never touched the damned gun.'

Bruce considered Asa. 'How'd you get shellacked?'

Again the deputy interrupted. 'Some fellers follered 'em out of the saloon, when the feller went down they come for Asa like a pack of wolves. If me'n the sheriff hadn't been there they'd've killed him.' Lange sighed. 'Now they're talkin' lynchin'. With the sheriff gone you know where that puts me? Hell, Bruce, I know every man-jack in my town. They're not goin' to lynch him nor anyone else. If they'd killed him . . . but they didn't. So now I'm alone sittin' on a powder barrel with a short lit fuse.'

Bruce considered the deputy. They had been friends for years. He finally said, 'Bud, the riders from Battleboro'll pen our drive in a day or two an' you know what comes next.'

Lange ponderously nodded. That was what happened at the end of every drive; after the cattle had been penned the drovers headed for the first saloon they came to. Under normal conditions there were fights. What Bud Lange could envision this time was a damned war.

He said, 'Who's head In'ian, Bruce?'

'Bentley Clavenger.'

The deputy sagged in his chair, considered his hands atop the desk briefly before saying, 'My brother told me I was crazy to hire on with the law in a shipping town. He was right. On your feet, Asa.'

After locking young Tucker in his cell, Deputy Lange returned to the office, flung the key ring on a desk and turned to lean there looking at Bruce Evans.

'The circuit rider was here last week, which means he won't be back for maybe six, seven weeks. Bruce, if they can they'll storm in here, take him out an' hang him.'

'Our crew will be here in a day or two. All you got to do is keep a lid on things until — '

'You didn't hear a damned thing I said, did you? If anybody but old Clavenger was in charge of your drive . . . but I know that disagreeable, belligerent son of a bitch.'

The deputy returned to his desk, sat down, leaned back and spoke again. 'I can't let your crew come into town. Wait a minute, don't flare up at me. If I got to I'll call out the Barnum vigilantes. Your crew'll sure as hell be troublesome. All I'm tryin' to do is keep a distance between us an' them.'

Bruce said, 'They been nearly four days drivin' cattle, an' in the damned rain. Bustin' loose in Barnum is what they always do an' it's what they look forward to. Bud, you call out your vigilantes and sure as hell there'll be a fight.'

'Keep 'em out of town, Bruce . . . please.'

Evans went as far as the door before speaking again. 'You got a doctor in Barnum?'

'We got one. When he's sober. I already had him look young Tucker over. He's bruised, but the medicine man said there warn't no broken bones, just that he got hit in the belly so often he won't have much appetite for a few days. Bruce, figure some way to keep your men out of town . . . Clavenger . . . I got an idea. When he comes stormin' in here I'll throw him in a cell for disturbin' the peace or whatever I can figure, an' you know what? I'll have me a hostage. Your riders stay out of town an' I'll release him. If they come stormin' in here you tell 'em I said Clavenger'll likely get shot tryin' to escape.'

Bruce said, 'And what about Asa?'

'I never lost a prisoner yet. I don't want to do it, but if lynchers show up I'll pepper 'em with bird shot.' The deputy wagged his head. 'What'd I do to deserve this mess?'

Bruce asked about the cattle awaiting shipment. The answer was normal for the circumstances. 'You know Mac Hutchinson? He runs cattle on the reservation an' pays in beef. Them's his cattle. They'll be gone by tomorrow afternoon. The cattle cars're due in the morning.' For a moment Deputy Lange was quiet then he said, 'I'll send some riders out to watch your drive.' As Bruce was lifting the draw string to the roadway door the deputy also said, 'They can't come into town, Bruce.'

4

A Killing

When Bruce returned, old Clavenger was waiting with the expression of someone who had been drinking vinegar. Bruce was dog-ass tired. While off-saddling he told the older man what had happened in Barnum and what the consequences were. As his animal was being led away he looked straight at Clavenger and said, 'We won't be allowed in town.'

The older man's colour slowly heightened. 'Who said that?'

'Deputy Sheriff Bud Lange.'

'Where's the sheriff?'

'Gone off somewhere to visit kin.'

'Well now! No gawddamned tinhorn deputy sheriff'll tell me what I can an' can't do.'

Bruce watched riders coming in to be replaced by other riders when he said, 'Bent, I got more trouble than I need without you makin' more. That's Hutchinson's cattle in the pens. The cars'll be in tomorrow to haul his cattle away. In the afternoon we can take our herd down there an' pen it. Then we're goin' out a ways, make camp an' stay out of town.'

The tough old cowman glared. 'That goes for the Tucker riders. You'll never see the day when you can tell me what I got to do. Bruce, this Tucker business ain't your affair. Asa's always been goin' off on a short fuse. Why'n't you just let it go?'

Evans regarded the older man. 'Old Birch was like a pa to me when I came here.'

'He's dead!'

'That don't mean I still don't owe him.'

Clavenger said, 'You're hopeless,' and went in the direction of the fire.

It was a fact that folks who knew each other pretty well could sense tensions. When Bruce came to the fire and sat between taciturn Walter Corrigan and Alamo Taunton, they exchanged a look behind Bruce's back and acted as though no tension existed.

He told them where Asa was and why he was there. Alamo wasn't as shocked as Corrigan was. He said, 'Dead drunk?'

Bruce sipped hot black coffee before speaking. 'That's the story. Asa pretty much agreed the feller was drunk.'

Walter Corrigan went to work methodically fashioning a smoke which he lighted from a firebrand and characteristically remained silent.

Alamo was quiet too but in a different way. He'd known Asa many riding seasons, if Asa killed a drunk the son of a bitch had it coming. He nudged Bruce, 'How do we get him out'n there?'

Bruce didn't answer. Busting Asa out of jail would simply add another burden on Bruce Evans. He and Bud Lange had been friends a long time.

As he arose to hunt up his soogans

he leaned and softly, quietly addressed Alamo. 'We don't bust him out.'

In the pre-dawn cold as the men were rigging out, Bruce noticed something. Clavenger's riders were cool. Evidently old Bent had spun his tale last night and because rangemen were traditionally and historically loyal to the brand they rode for they favoured their employer's attitude, and when Bruce was swinging across leather he looked for Bent Clavenger. It was dark, there was considerable milling; he didn't see him, which didn't mean much at the time. After eating and before getting astride most men hunkered close to a tree or a wagon wheel out of sight somewhere and peed.

They were ready to ride out and bring back any nocturnal strays when Bob Whitney called for Bent and got no answer. It really didn't matter; they wouldn't need the point rider until later. Bob gave it up, rode with the others, joined them in splitting into two groups, each group to make a half surround sweep and bring back drifters if they found any.

Clavenger's riders joined the easterly split. It made the split lopsided but no one said anything. When Bruce and his split were making a wide sweep west to east Walter Corrigan came up and said, 'The old man went toward Barnum coupla hours before we rolled out.' At the look he got from Evans he also said, 'He pussy-footed for a fair distance then busted over into a lope. It was hard to see but sound carries. He was goin' to the town.'

Corrigan dropped back to his place in the sweep and Bruce neither spoke nor disassociated himself from the gather until the few head they had found had been drifted back to the rest of the herd, then he hunted up Bob Whitney, jerked his head and when they were beyond earshot of the others he said, 'Old Bent left out in the dark in the direction of Barnum.'

Whitney was having a toothpick for breakfast and spat it out before saying,

'He'll make trouble sure as I'm standin' here.'

That remark was too obvious to earn a response so when next Bruce spoke it was on a different subject.

'Ride over and see if the pens are empty. There was supposed to be a train in this morning. If they're still loading come on back an' we'll drift the herd slowly in that direction.' When Whitney gave Evans an odd look the cowman said, 'We got to get rid of the cattle first, Bob.'

Whitney left in the direction of Barnum. Bruce told a Clavenger rider named Simmons to ride point. Simmons stood his ground. 'Bent told us to stay in camp until he got back.'

Bruce gave the Clavenger rider stare for stare when he said, 'Then you boys off-saddle and make yourselves comfortable. We're goin' to start a slow drift toward Barnum.'

Simmons got the other Clavenger riders together and told them what Evans had said. One rangeman said,

'If the herd's moved who's to mind the Clavenger critters?'

Another Clavenger rider spoke. This man was an old hand, lined, tough and businesslike. 'Damned if we hang back, an' we'll most likely get fired if we go with the drive. Me; I been fired before. I don't care much for Mr Clavenger but damned if I'm goin' to stay here because sure as hell bein' short-handed they'll lose cattle.'

Clavenger had three riders. Two of them were surly but they went with the snail-paced drive. One of them was Simmons, the other one was named Knolton. One man stayed behind according to orders.

Taking their time allowed the cattle to spread out some and graze along, which was perfectly agreeable with them. Keeping them from widening their grazing route too far the riders yielded up to a point. Beyond that point they choused the animals back.

The sun was rising when Bob Whitney appeared in the middle

distance approaching at an easy lope. Bruce went ahead. Where they met rooftops were in sight. Whitney said, 'Directly you'll hear the train pull out.' Whitney looked past, saw the leisurely approaching cattle and sighed. He would have waited to make certain first that the pens were empty. All he said was, 'The town seemed normal. There wasn't no sign of the old man but I didn't ride on in.'

Evans sent Whitney back to make sure the gates were wide open and to position himself so that spooked critters couldn't bypass the gates and bolt.

With Alamo Taunton riding point and Corrigan on the north wing beginning to bend the cattle southward, Bruce rode up beside that weathered and seasoned Clavenger rider and said, 'The old man had ought to thank you for lookin' after his interest.'

The older man looked straight at Bruce when he bluntly said, 'He won't. He'll fire me.' He gestured. 'Someone's comin' from town.'

There was no mistaking the rider even at a considerable distance. Bruce was wheeling away when he said, 'The law.'

It was too early for sweat but the big deputy was sweating. He neglected one of the customary greetings to say, 'Why'd you let old Bent Clavenger come to town?'

'I didn't let the old bastard do anythin'. He snuck away in the dark. Did you jail him?'

'Jail him! It'd be easier to jail a catamount. He bought breakfast at the eatery and talked up trouble. I wasn't there, but some fellers told me he said anyone who committed cold-blooded murder had ought to be hung.'

'What'd you do, Bud?'

'Went lookin' for him but he rode out of town. Bruce, if he comes back here you grab the old bastard . . . you got chains? Chain him up an' keep him out of town.'

'That's your job, Bud.'

The large man's pale eyes flashed

fire. 'If I see him I'll do it but if he comes back here . . . '

'All right. There'll likely be a fight, he's got riders with the drive.'

Deputy Lange's brow acquired two wide, deep creases before he said, 'I'm goin' back to town. One of us'll find him. If you get trouble fire off a couple of shots. I'll have the vigilantes rounded up. We'll come a-running.'

As Bruce watched the big man lope back in the direction from which he had come he shook his head. Any man who weighed over 200 pounds had no business riding a 900-pound horse.

He remained on the south side. Alamo was nearing the pens. Riders were drifting forward on the north side but if there were bunch-quitters in the drive they didn't offer to run for it.

The train was pulling out. Its noise made the cattle uncomfortable but they walked head to tail into the pens. The train was a quarter-mile along when its whistle was blown.

In open country that would have

started a stampede. Corralled animals milled, struck log stringers, rammed one another and bawled.

Alamo was closing and chaining gates; he and the wiry Clavenger rider. Alamo looked after the train and yelled to the older man, 'If you'll catch an' hold that whistle-blowin' son of a bitch I'll kill him.'

Bruce swung down, leaned both arms across his saddle seat and wagged his head. He too would have liked to have ten minutes with the whistle-blower. If he'd blown his whistle fifteen minutes earlier there would have been stampeding cattle in every direction.

He turned to watch the drag riders dismount to roll and light smokes. Behind them some yards, a horse and rider were approaching. He didn't recognize the rider but he knew Birch Tucker's Morgan horse.

Clavenger rode wide around heading in the direction of the cattle pens. Bruce watched him. The old man looked neither right nor left.

When he was close enough he called to the weathered older rangeman, 'Piñon, you son of a bitch, I said for you fellers to stay in camp.'

There was a time to call a man a son of a bitch and a time not to. It was a common insult among old friends who were smiling. The leathery man Clavenger had addressed stood briefly leaning on a closed gate in silence. Then he moved without haste toward Bentley Clavenger who anticipated his purpose and swapped ends of his shot-loaded quirt and waited until his rider was close enough to grab the bridle of his horse and called the rider every fierce name he knew.

His voice carried. There were other men, mostly on the ground but a few still a-horseback. Not a one of them moved nor made a sound.

Clavenger finished swearing and said, 'Take your hand off that bridle or so help me Gawd I'll bust your skull!'

The man Clavenger had called Piñon

71

didn't release the bridle, he swung the horse's head away from him. When the horse moved clear Piñon lunged and Clavenger swung.

A shot-loaded quirt can kill a horse if it's used right. Piñon wasn't a horse, he was clearly experienced and seasoned. He didn't try to dodge the quirt, he used his left forearm to block it and at the same time grabbed the old man's loosely-worn shellbelt and threw himself backward as hard as he could.

Clavenger squawked, fought to grab the horn, missed, lost his seat and fell.

Piñon didn't use his left arm, it was broken. When Clavenger rolled to get up Piñon kicked him hard. The old man squawked again and curled like a ball.

Piñon leaned out, yanked the quirt loose from Clavenger's wrist, straightened up and swung it. The sound of lead-loaded leather striking bone was loud enough for all but the most distant riders to hear.

Bruce left his horse standing. Piñon turned, still gripping the quirt. He said, 'I got no fight with you, Mr Evans.'

Bruce went past, stood looking down for a long moment before facing around. Piñon hadn't moved. Bruce dug in a pocket, pulled out a roll of greenbacks, Piñon took them in his right hand, dropped the quirt, went to his horse and mounted without gripping the horn, got astride and said, 'I'm right obliged, Mr Evans.'

'You better get that arm tended to.'

'I will, it's been broke before. Thanks again.'

Piñon broke over into a loose lope riding southward.

Bruce leaned, placed Clavenger's hat over his face and as he was straightening up the riders converged. One of them softly said, 'Dead . . . ?'

Bruce nodded. Another rangeman picked up the quirt and hefted it, shook his head and handed it to someone else.

The solitary remaining Clavenger

rider needed something to lean on, went to the nearest corral, looked at the others and said, 'If you'll help, I'll load him on his horse an' take him back.'

Bruce shook his head. 'That horse don't belong to him. It stays with me.'

'How'll I get him back to camp?'

Alamo Taunton growled a reply, 'Carry the son of a bitch.'

The Clavenger rider didn't have to do that. Two buggies were coming from the direction of town. Behind them, partially hidden, was the beefy big deputy on his — for him — undersized horse.

It looked like two men in the first buggy, one man in the second rig. The 'man' in the foremost buggy was a woman.

The buggies halted where the rangemen were standing. The driver was a grey-headed unsmiling man wearing a badge on the lapel of his coat. He dropped a tether weight, reset his hat and said, 'Mister Evans?'

Bruce nodded. They were barely acquainted but he knew the greying man was the county sheriff, Will Holt. Bruce brushed the brim of his hat to the woman. Mistaking her for a man at a distance in a buggy was understandable. She was wearing a stockman's beaver-belly Stetson hat.

She wasn't young, possibly forty-five or fifty. Her hair and eyes were coal black, her colouring was very light tan. She was attractive without being pretty and had a set to her jaw a bulldog would have envied.

She didn't give the lawman a chance to introduce her. She walked up to Bruce Evans, held out a hand and introduced herself. 'Maryanne Holt.'

Bruce smiled. 'Bruce Evans.'

The woman was still holding Bruce's hand when two rangemen moved and she saw the dead man.

Bud Lange came up last. He and a bird-built man wearing a curly brim derby hat and matching coat and britches stopped side by side. The deputy went to lift the hat and drop it back over Clavenger's head. He addressed the sheriff. 'He's here . . . dead, Sheriff.'

Lange stood with the trim, expressionless county sheriff looking down. The sheriff turned. 'What happened?'

Alamo Taunton replied in a dry drawl. 'Fell off his horse, broke his neck I'd guess.'

The lawman stooped lifted the hat and while still leaning said, 'He must've hit pretty hard. Looks like he busted his head.'

Taunton agreed using the same matter-of-fact tone. 'It looks like that's what he done for a fact.'

The stranger wearing the elegant hat joined the others in considering the dead man. He eventually said, 'Well, you don't need me out here, Sheriff,' and turned so abruptly he bumped Bruce Evans. He apologized then introduced himself. 'Jerome White, Mayor of Barnum. I also do embalmin' an' buryin'. If you need my services . . . '

Bruce interrupted. 'What we need is some way to get his carcass back to our camp east of here.'

His Honour was short. 'See the liveryman in town,' he said, and would have walked to his rig but the sheriff stopped him.

'You can do it, Jerry. They'll likely pay. We'll load him in the buggy for you,' the sheriff said, sounding curt.

Bruce didn't help but others did. His Honour lost colour and stammered but when the sheriff came toward him His Honour moved past, climbed into the buggy and asked directions. That uncomfortable Clavenger rider said, 'Follow me,' got his horse and rode off without looking back.

Bud Lange sidled up close to Bruce Evans to speak in a low voice, nodding curtly in the sheriff's direction as he said, 'What he come out here for is about young Tucker.'

Bruce nodded. 'I figured it'd be

something like that.'

'When he gets around to it he'll tell you no riders connected with your drive can enter town. He's dead set on holding Birch's brother for killin' that drunk.'

'That horse thief you mean.'

Lange shrugged. 'I got no ideas about that. Neither does the sheriff. Bruce, you want some advice?'

'Maybe. What is it?'

'Go home, take the riders an' go back.'

Evans frowned. 'That'll leave Asa likely to get hanged.'

'Not without a trial when the circuit-ridin' judge gets back.'

Bruce considered the larger man and slowly shook his head. Possibly the deputy had anticipated this because he said, 'You can't come into town so you might as well go home. Young Tucker'll stay put until the judge gets back. He'll get a fair trial.'

'Bud . . . is he a hangin' judge?'

Lange's gaze fled and returned and

Bruce Evans showed a tight, wry smile. He said, 'Partner, tell the missus hello for me,' and walked away.

He was heading for his horse when the woman wearing a rangeman's Stetson interrupted his walk by stopping and facing Bruce when she said, 'That lad in jail is your kin?'

Bruce stopped. 'No, ma'am. Not blood kin. His pa was like a father to me an' I knew his boys since way back, an' that includes the one in the jailhouse.'

The woman's rock-set jaw loosened slightly. 'Loyalty,' she softly said, and let her voice harden. 'Doesn't seem much doubt the man he shot couldn't protect himself.'

'Ma'am, don't get mad; what's your interest?'

'The sheriff is my stepfather. My father was Alex Weathers. He died when I was nine years old.'

'An' you live in Barnum?'

'No. I visit Barnum as often as I can. I was born and grew up here. I live in

Fort Collins. That's where I have my practice.'

Bruce was impressed. He'd never before met a female doctor. He relaxed slightly. 'Sort of keep your pa healthy?'

She looked blank. 'He keeps himself healthy. My mother sees to that.'

Bruce tried again, lamely. 'Are you figurin' to move your practice to Barnum? Seems to me it'd hardly pay. Not enough folks get sick in this country.'

Her eyes widened. 'I'm not a physician, Mr Evans. I'm a lawyer.'

This time Bruce's surprise showed. He'd never met a female lawyer before. He'd heard of them but they were rare in a man's world.

5

Retaliation

Sheriff Holt was a terse man, not without understanding and humour but not under the present circumstances. When Bruce mentioned Asa Tucker the lawman spoke in an unequivocal tone of voice. 'Your riders stay clear of town. I won't have no trouble stirred up. No more than I already got.' The sheriff looked at Alamo Taunton. 'That feller is trouble. I know him from ten years back. He stayed out of prison in west Texas by the skin of his teeth.'

Alamo smiled. 'Good to see you again, Will.'

The sheriff ignored that as he faced Bruce. 'Let's co-operate, Mr Evans. You penned your drive, you got no other business in the Barnum country so just go back.'

Bruce didn't interrupt, but after the lawman finished he said, 'You got lynchers in Barnum, Sheriff, an' your prisoner is family to me.'

'He'll get a fair trial,' the sheriff said. 'There won't be any lynchin'. I never let one happen yet . . . Mr Evans, go home an' leave the rest to me.'

Bruce quietly said, 'I can't do that. Not with young Tucker in jail an' Barnum full of lynch talk.'

The woman wearing the beaver-belly Stetson hat came up and smiled at the sheriff. 'I represent Asa Tucker.'

The sheriff was momentarily shocked and speechless. His daughter took full advantage of his silence. 'My client was paying back for the horse thief shooting his brother.'

'What horse thief, Maryanne?'

'His name was Red Arnold and he shot Birch Tucker, left him for dead, took his horse to Battleboro and sold it for twenty-five dollars. It's a Morgan horse. Young Tucker found Red Arnold. He didn't find Arnold's horse-stealing partner, a man named Bonner Watkins.'

The sheriff said, 'Who've you been talking to?'

His daughter widely smiled. 'You prevent a lynching, I've got work to do. See you in court, Dad.'

His Honour's buggy with its dead passenger was distant, the corralled cattle had tanked up at the trough and were now hungry. They paced restlessly. For all but the culls this was the first time they had been held for any great length of time in an enclosure. Cattle lack some of being smart but they have instincts. Right now they had a premonition and it made them restless.

Bruce, his friends from the Battleboro country and the men from Barnum watched the female lawyer head for town. The sheriff faced Bruce Evans. 'She don't belong here. She's got a — '

'Acts like she belongs now, Sheriff. Asa needs a lawyer.' As Bruce finished speaking the sheriff dolorously wagged his head: a simple case of chousin' away some drovers had become something else.

He addressed his bulky deputy. 'Bud, go back. Don't let Maryanne talk to young Tucker.'

As Bud was turning, Bruce stopped him. 'He's got a right to see a lawyer, Bud, same as any other prisoner has.'

The deputy, caught between them, looked at the sheriff for whatever was said next.

It was said but not for an extraordinary length of time. The sheriff was stumped and showed it. Eventually he told his deputy he could go back to town but to ignore that business of preventing the prisoner from talking to anyone.

The drive was corralled, all that was now required was a skeleton crew to help with the loading and since there would not be another cattle train along until the following day the Clavenger riders along with rangemen belonging to other outfits were anxious to get home.

The men milled and mumbled. There were some willing to remain behind with the Ox Shoe and Tucker riders. Bruce discouraged this. He was confident, at least he left that impression, so some of the rangemen headed back to the wagon camp.

Bob Whitney mentioned eating; it had been a long day. Bruce looked toward the town. Despite being ordered not to enter Barnum there was the matter of eating. Alamo Taunton offered to ride in alone, get fed and return.

Bruce nodded. He and the others watched Alamo all the way to the north end of Barnum.

There was nothing to do. There was water at the trough but it was a poor substitute for cooked meat.

They discussed the killing of old man Clavenger. No one missed having him around nor did anyone think the rider called Piñon hadn't given Clavenger his deserts.

The sun was low and beginning

to discolour before they saw a rider approaching from town. Walter Corrigan said, 'That's not Alamo,' and he was right, it was the big beefy deputy looking as solemn as an owl. When he dismounted he said, 'Mister Holt locked him up.'

'Alamo?'

Bud Lange nodded.

'What for?'

'He didn't say. He seen him goin' into the café, went over, disarmed Alamo, marched him to the jailhouse and locked him in the same cell with Asa.'

That lacked a lot of the kind of explanation the rangemen wanted. Someone growled. 'Let's go get him.'

No one picked up on that immediately. It wasn't just the sheriff with one deputy, it was the mood of the town.

Bruce asked if the lynch talk had died down and the deputy shook his head as he said, 'Old Holt's girl's with Asa.'

That did not impress anyone.

Further discussion was interrupted by a rider coming from the direction of the wagon camp. He was a Clavenger rider named Al Hopper. He was a 'breed, dark with matching jet-black hair and eyes. He'd been a Clavenger top hand.

The others waited without speaking and moving until Hopper came up, swung to the ground and said, 'That old man was a miserable bastard,' and having expressed himself about Clavenger, he said, 'With him dead there's no reason for me to go back so I kind of thought if you gents was shorthanded . . . '

Walter Corrigan spoke before anyone else could. 'You're plumb welcome. They got Alamo in the jailhouse yonder.'

'What'd he do?'

'Rode into town to get fed. He was hungry.'

Bruce put that statement into perspective. 'The sheriff said none of us can go into Barnum.'

The black-eyed 'breed turned his head. 'Gents, I'm hungry, too,' mounted his horse and without another word rode toward the town.

Bruce had an idea about that. 'They won't know him down there,' and he was right.

Al Hopper left his animal to be grained at the livery barn, found an eatery and went inside. The proprietor, like others, was not fond of Indians but he served up a meal.

The people of Barnum might have appeared to be going about their business normally but they knew as long as Sheriff Holt had one of the cowmen in his jailhouse, and as long as those visible rangemen out yonder were not leaving, the inevitable result would be trouble.

They were prepared, the local vigilante group had been called up. People who were not associated with either law enforcement or the vigilance committee had reason to expect trouble and were in one way or another prepared for it.

The 'breed finished his supper, went out front to roll and light a smoke and four men converged, two from the south, two from the north. One of them, a squatty, bull-built individual addressed Al Hopper.

'You with them rangemen out yonder?'

Hopper dropped his smoke and stamped on it before answering. 'I guess so. At least I helped drive the cattle down here. Why?'

Another man, lanky with a tipped-down hat that hid his eyes spoke next. 'I seen you out there with 'em. You fellers was told you wasn't to come into town.'

Hopper showed no anxiety. 'I was hungry an' there's no way to get fed out there.'

The bull-built man said, 'Shuck your pistol!'

The 'breed faced the shorter but more massive townsman. 'I told you, there's nothin' to eat out there.'

'*Shuck the gun!*'

Hopper tugged the tie down loose,

lifted out his sixgun and dropped it. Two of the townsmen noticeably loosened. The bull-built man said, 'Cross over an' stop in front of the jailhouse.'

Again Hopper obeyed. As the little troop crossed the road with watchers at most windows he stepped up on to the plankwalk and turned south. Two of the townsmen turned back evidently satisfied. The massive man and a gangling younger man walked behind the 'breed. When they came to a trash-laden vacant space between two buildings with weeds nearly waist high Hopper paused and turned to speak. 'What're you chargin' me with?' he asked.

The gangling man seemed to have lost the ability to speak but the other man hadn't and he was closest when he said, 'Bein' where you was told not to be.'

Hopper stopped stone still. 'Is that a law?' he asked, and the massively muscular man replied irritably. 'For you it is. Just keep walkin'.' To emphasize this order the man reached to shove the 'breed.

Hopper didn't swing from the waist, he shot his fist overhand from the shoulder as straight and hard as a battering ram.

The burly man went down like a pole-axed steer and his companion was too stunned to move as Hopper hurled himself from the plankwalk into the overgrown bit of land running like a deer.

Someone across the road fired a wild shot. Moments later the pursuit was in full force. Barnum's vigilantes were capable men. If there was an advantage they knew their town. There was another advantage, Indians were particularly adept at becoming invisible in places with any kind of cover available.

They heard the gunshot out where the rangemen were waiting. Bruce flung out a hand when Walter Corrigan and another man started forward. When

Bruce growled the man with Corrigan said, 'They'll kill him!'

Bruce's reply was given in a dry tone of voice. 'Not unless they can see in the dark,' and he was right but the 'breed did not get back among friends for more than an hour. He hadn't dared go to the livery barn for his horse.

Like most rangemen he was not fond of walking and the hike back had pretty well tired him, but he smiled when he said, 'They just plain don't like folks down there.'

Bruce's dilemma was that he could not abandon Alamo Taunton nor Birch's brother. With daylight dying he proposed that they go down there on foot, catch the sheriff or his deputy before they closed up for the night, get Asa and Alamo and hustle back for their horses and be gone before daylight.

It was a basic idea; if Bruce hadn't mentioned it someone else surely would have.

They waited until night was down, stars shone and the moon either hadn't arrived or was in a cycle which meant when and if it did return it would be too skinny to provide much light.

Bruce led off. It wasn't difficult gauging directions nor distances. With one or two exceptions every one of them had been in Barnum before.

Al Hopper, whose forefathers had been accomplished horse and woman thieves either had taught their techniques to the 'breed or he had inherited the knowledge; in either case he scouted ahead, which was rewarding. He saw the two night watchers from his belly-down position and watched them. Both townsmen were armed with saddle guns as well as belt-guns. Neither of them seemed alert but rather bored. Hopper heard one tell the other vigilante it was crazy for the sheriff to take all these precautions; at best there wasn't more'n five, six rangemen.

Hopper back-crawled until he could arise then he went back and told the others what he'd found. When asked if he could find those two watchers again Hopper grinned, 'Like a homin' pigeon.'

He led the way, stayed out in front until he smelled tobacco smoke then stealthily crouched. One of the watchers was gone, the other one was still where they had been.

Hopper went back to enlighten Evans and Bruce thought they should capture the remaining man. As they went forward this time they fanned out until the indolent vigilante was surrounded, then Bruce told the 'breed to emulate an owl which Hopper did. The sentinel straightened up, peering in the direction of the owl hoot.

Bob Whitney came silently up behind the man and softly spoke to him. 'No noise, mister. Drop the Winchester an' the belt-gun. I said *no noise!*'

The watcher had scuffed his feet as he partially turned in the direction of Whitney's voice. He stopped moving and very carefully shucked his weapons, then he said, 'You danged idiot, the whole town's waitin'.'

They went further back with their hostage who turned out to be the bull-built local blacksmith. He and Al Hopper had met before and the 'breed showed a row of perfect white teeth when the burly man recognized him.

The blacksmith wasn't intimidated, he scornfully said, 'Sheriff Holt was a rangeman. He figured what you'd do. Barnum's got armed men in just about every doorway and hid around the jailhouse. You boys be interested in a little advice?'

Bruce nodded.

'Get on your horses an' don't even look back. Come daylight the sheriff's goin' to come for you with a posse.'

Bruce jerked his head for the man to be taken away, gagged, bound and left where he could neither get upright, walk, nor yell.

The blacksmith protested every inch of the way. He mentioned the number of vigilantes waiting down yonder and their order from the sheriff to shoot to kill anyone approaching his jailhouse.

His captors went about their work of incapacitating him without a word. As they walked away he cursed them through his gag.

The only remark made about the captive was made by Al Hopper who thought the blacksmith could whip his weight in mountain lions. No one commented; he probably could.

They were part way back toward town staying to the west side when someone down there blew a whistle and Bob Whitney sighed. He'd been a vigilante; he knew how they used whistles at night to transmit orders by whistle code.

Bruce Evans halted only when he was close enough to see an occasional shadow dart from one place of concealment to another.

There were few lights showing and most of them were from lamps in residences. The main thoroughfare was as dark as the inside of a boot.

To reach the alley behind the jailhouse they would have to move stealthily between residences on the west side and darkened stores on the east side.

Walter Corrigan was of the opinion that going down that alley would put them between armed gunmen in both directions. Bruce agreed. Whatever one thought of the sheriff he had to be given his due; anticipating an attempted jail break he would make the approach from any direction as good as possible.

They reached the alley from the north and halted. The 'breed said he could smell an ambush. That was good enough. Bruce led the way back northward to the edge of Barnum, crossed to the east side and led the way in among houses, mostly unkempt and unpainted except for a handsome two-storey large house with an array of flowers out front behind a picket fence.

They had to work their way some distance to locate the back alley's entrance. Bruce sent Hopper to scout.

He returned wagging his head. 'One old dog, likely deef. Nothin' else. Who lives in that big house?'

'Feller named Bartlett who owns the general store. Andy Bartlett. Let's go.'

They were as silent as possible up until they climbed the back porch and the planks squeaked. Bruce growled, 'Stay to the far edges.'

The door was bolted, not as was customary with a *tranca* that fitted into a pair of hangers on the inside but with one of those new fangled city locks that operated with a key.

Trancas were virtually indestructible. They could not be forced from the outside. Those town locks could be forced.

Without a word Walter Corrigan crouched in front of the lock. What he did was hidden from the others until he straightened up and gave the door a gentle push. The scent of a meal still lingered, it reminded the rangemen they hadn't been fed. One of them would have plundered a cupboard but someone growled at him.

The parlour was opulently furnished. It had rugs covering most of the boards and the same variety of carpeting went up the stairwell.

It was darker inside than it was outside. They had to grope their way and be noiseless. Their reward was the sound of a man snoring with trumpet regularity. Bruce led the way past the landing, eased a door open and paused as the snoring passed from higher-pitched racket to a sound of wet gurglings.

Bruce led the way. There were two people in the bed, both were wearing night caps but the woman's head covering fitted snugly while the headpiece of her husband was a tasseled night cap to keep a bald head warm.

Bruce gestured toward the lamp on a bedside table. Bob Whitney raised the mantle, applied a match to the wick, lowered the mantle, turned up the wick and stepped back. The room was fully brightened.

The woman awakened first, rolled her eyes and placed a hand on her husband's chest and lightly drummed. The man awakened, irritably brushed the tassel of his night cap out of his face, stared and slowly pushed himself into a sitting position. When being stunned passed he said, 'What're you doin' in my house?'

In acceptance with the tenet that a stupid question deserved a stupid answer Bruce replied.

'My name's Bruce Evans from over around Battleboro. We delivered cattle to the railroad pens. Your sheriff's got two of our friends. You're goin' to help us get 'em out.'

The portly individual pushed himself straighter in the bed and darkly scowled. 'You got the wrong house. Sheriff Holt lives — '

'Get up an' get dressed, mister. We're goin' to do some horse tradin'. You'n a hefty built feller we got out yonder. The trade'll be even up. You'n the hefty feller for our two fellers in the jailhouse.'

The woman made a slight whimpering sound which annoyed her husband. He turned still glowering. 'Be quiet, Emma.' He faced the rangemen again, 'I'm not goin' to help you do no such a thing. I'll be damned first. Get out of my house!'

Bruce winked at Al Hopper who started for the woman's side of the bed. He yanked her night cap off, pulled a wicked bladed boot knife and straightened up with it as he said, 'I never took no scalps. My pa did an' my grandpa but I never have . . . hold still woman!'

She fainted and her husband reached across to grab the 'breed. Hopper nimbly stepped back, raised his knife arm and said, 'That's right decent of you, tryin' to protect her. How much hair you got?'

Hopper snatched off the night cap, dropped it and curled his lip, the merchant didn't have enough on top to take hold of during a scalping.

Bruce Evans stepped between them. 'Get your clothes on. *Now!*' He yanked the covers back. Walter Corrigan went around to the far side of the bed, drew his six-gun and cocked it.

The storekeeper got out of bed, dressed quickly and looked at his wife who was staring at him. In a different tone of voice he said, 'Things'll be fine, Emma. I'll be back directly.'

She did not speak nor move except her eyes. She watched her husband being herded out of the room.

When they were outside in the dark alley the merchant said, 'Where are we going?'

Bruce answered curtly. 'Don't talk, just follow the In'ian.'

It was quite a hike on a chilly night for an older man but he followed Hopper without a word. When they got back where they'd started and the storekeeper saw the town blacksmith tied and silently glaring, he faced Bruce.

'How much do you want?'

Bruce gestured. 'Sit down an' shut up.'

They tied the storekeeper and hunkered. Dawn would be along in a few hours. Bruce told Bob Whitney and Walter Corrigan he normally didn't favour lynching but if the sheriff didn't turn Alamo and Asa loose he'd favour hanging both hostages in plain sight of the town.

Corrigan, who rarely smiled and almost never spoke, did both. 'What happened to all them vigilantes supposed to be watchin' for us?'

The 'breed Indian reminded them of something they'd overlooked when he said, 'That caféman turns out one hell of a supper.'

No one commented. It had been so long since the others had eaten, their stomachs thought their throats had been cut.

6

The Female Fee Lawyer

When daylight arrived there was an obvious degree of agitated order in the town. Two women were responsible, the wives of the storekeeper and the blacksmith.

While the inhabitants of Barnum were breakfasting, two horsemen left riding north at a steady, slow gait and Bob Whitney thought they were as glum and grim-looking pair of individuals he'd seen in some time.

It turned out to be a correct notion. Sheriff Holt and his beefy deputy did not raise the wave which was customary, they rode where Bruce was standing and dismounted. The deputy held the reins while the sheriff addressed Evans.

'Are you goin' to turn 'em loose or

do I have to round up the vigilantes, outnumber you four to one and come out and arrest the lot of you?'

Evans said, 'Turn who loose?' and the sheriff's face reddened. He was not a patient man.

'The storekeeper an' the blacksmith.'

Bruce nodded. 'We'll make a trade, Sheriff.'

'*No trade!* Get that through your head. I got a murderer an' he stays locked up until the circuit-riding judge gets back.'

Bruce loosened his stance. 'Sheriff, we're goin' to hang 'em unless you trade, in plain sight of the town.'

The sheriff's grim expression said all there was to say.

The sheriff turned, retrieved his reins, swung across leather and sat a moment looking at Bruce Evans before reining back the way he had come.

His deputy glanced back long enough to show a forlorn expression. They watched them head for town and the 'breed Indian said, 'How many vigilantes they got down there?'

No one replied because no one knew the answer.

Bruce was going to lose in this stand-off when it came to a real confrontation and knew it. It didn't matter how many townsmen would ride with the sheriff, any number higher than five would be too many.

A solitary horseman approaching from the northeast on a loose rein wasn't noticed until someone turned and saw him, and growled to the others.

When the stranger was close enough he raised his right arm palm forward and lowered it. Walt Corrigan returned the greeting but no one else did.

Hopper the 'breed stood like a statue frowning until he said, 'That's Claude Garret from town.'

He was correct and when the man from Battleboro was close enough to dismount, he addressed Bruce Evans in a drawling voice. 'Help's comin'. Clavenger's boys come back yesterday, told us what was goin' on over here an' folks made up a posse. I come ahead to sort of scout up things.'

Walt Corrigan said, 'How many?'

The man from Battleboro answered shortly. 'Eleven. Twelve countin' me.' He faced Bruce Evans again. 'If you'd tell me what this is all about I'll go back an' tell the others.'

Bruce started with the shooting and ended up with Sheriff Holt's threat to come out and use guns to settle things.

The lean, greying man named Garret swung astride, nodded around and turned to lope back the way he had come. For him it was a short ride. The rangemen with Bruce Evans saw the party of riders come up out of a swale no more than a quarter-mile away and watched Claude Garret meet them. They all halted while Garret talked, then resumed their approach.

Someone in Barnum whistled loudly. Bruce and his companions had their backs to the town and did not turn.

Whatever the whistle signified could be of concern to the townsmen down yonder but it meant nothing to the band of horsemen who were dismounting as the men on the ground began talking.

The sun was climbing, there was heat in the day and down yonder the roadway was deserted. One of the newcomers was Rory Kildare, the saloonman from Battleboro. After a squinty-eyed look southward he said, 'They're either gettin' set or they're climbin' under their beds.' As he paused to regard Bruce Evans he said, 'Did Asa really shoot someone in cold blood?'

Al Hopper, the 'breed, answered before Bruce could. 'He called the feller, they went out into the roadway and the feller wasn't good enough.'

Bob Whitney dryly said, 'They said the other feller was drunk, didn't have a chance.'

The townsmen had heard all they needed to hear. Several went to care for horses. Only two men had food in their saddle-bags.

They shared what they could which was just enough to aggravate empty stomachs.

Several mounted men appeared at the north end of Barnum. They sat like statues and the 'breed laughed.

He didn't laugh when four other riders met the first two and one of the men from Battleboro pointed. Three more horsemen appeared to join the six. Rory Kildare said, 'Well now, that's more like it,' and went to get a Winchester from his saddle boot.

The townsman whose saddle-bags had been emptied said, 'What'n hell they just settin' there for?' and taciturn Walter Corrigan answered unhappily. 'They're fixin' to starve us to death.'

Hopper the 'breed sounded disgusted when he spoke next. 'Let's get astride. Go down there an' if they want a fight — '

He was interrupted by Bob Whitney. 'Who in hell is that?'

Bruce answered him. 'I recognize the

109

hat, that's the sheriff's daughter.'

'Well for Chris'sake are they goin' to take a female woman to make war on us with?'

No one spoke as the mounted riders down yonder began heading north at a dead walk. Several townsmen went after their Winchesters, two other townsmen were worried that the approaching riders might cripple them in the best way to do it, by running off their saddle stock, and went out where the horses were.

Bruce rolled and lighted a smoke. A townsman standing nearby took his cue from this and cheeked a cud of eating tobacco.

When the riders were close enough Bruce Evans walked out to meet them. Bob Whitney and Rory Kildare followed. Kildare, the saloonman, who didn't like Indians, full blood or 'breeds, seemed to have forgotten his bias.

Sheriff Holt drew rein, rested both hands atop the saddle horn and sat gazing steadily at Bruce Evans without making a sound.

Bruce spoke first. 'Do you want to turn 'em loose, Mr Holt, or get off your horses an' join us in watchin' the hanging?'

Holt's daughter pushed her way through, drew rein looking steadily at Bruce. 'Under the law they can't be turned loose on a murder charge.'

Bruce returned her steady gaze. 'You rode out here to tell me that, ma'am?'

'No. I rode out here to tell you to go back where you came from. I have the sheriff's word nothing will happen to your friends.'

Bruce shook his head. 'Can't do that, ma'am. The sheriff's got a feller named Alamo Taunton locked up. He rode into town to get somethin' to eat. Is that a crime, ma'am?'

The sheriff spoke first in a bitter voice. 'You can have Taunton. All you got to do is let them hostages go back with us.'

'And Asa?'

'Maryanne just told you . . . you hard of hearing? For murder there's no bail an' no lettin' him go.'

Bruce looked among the townsmen. He might have met some of them on previous trips to Barnum but at the moment couldn't put a name to any of them.

Sheriff Holt had little patience. Expecting an answer which he hadn't got, he said, 'The lad'll get a decent trial. No one'll bother him between now'n then.'

'You got lynchers down there, Sheriff,' Evans said.

'I made it plain, anybody comes near my jailhouse night or day makin' lynch talk I'll shoot 'em on sight.' The sheriff paused making a faint frown. 'Did that feller young Tucker shot kill his brother?'

'Wounded him. As far as I know he's still alive. Shot him to steal his Morgan horse an' left him for dead. I'd say that's cause enough to find the feller, Sheriff.'

'No argument there, Mr Evans. It's how he done it. That sorrel-headed feller'd been drinkin' for an hour. Folks from the saloon said he was gettin' orry eyed.'

'Asa called him an' they went out into the road, Sheriff.'

Maryanne Holt spoke up. 'Half the men in the saloon said he was drunk, Mr Evans.'

'Ma'am, I thought you was on Asa's side.'

'I am. It was second-degree murder. That's not a hanging offence.'

'Prison, Ma'am?'

'That'd be up to the judge.'

Bruce sighed and wagged his head. 'Suppose I put up bond an' take him home?'

'Didn't you hear what the sheriff told you? There's no bail on a murder charge.'

'Well then, ma'am, you'n your pa and these other gents can turn around and go back where you come from.'

Sheriff Holt had been following this

exchange and darkly said, 'You're goin'
to set out here'n hatch meanness to get
that boy out of my jailhouse. I told
you; anyone comes near'll get shot.
Now you come ahead.'

Sheriff Holt turned, jerked his head
for the townsmen to follow, and headed
back toward Barnum. His daughter
lingered, got down from her horse and
spoke directly to Bruce Evans.

'He won't be lynched, I can promise
you that.'

'That's right decent of you, ma'am,
because if Asa gets lynched we're goin'
to ride into town and have our own
necktie party, startin' with the sheriff.'

She flared out at him. 'Don't talk
like that! Your way is only going to
make matters worse.'

'What other way is there, ma'am?'

She didn't answer, she turned, got
astride and turned back.

One of the Battleboro townsmen
said, 'Mister Evans, they'll send for
the army.'

Walter Corrigan had the answer to

that. 'The nearest army post's at Fort Laramie. Whatever happens here will be over'n done with before soldiers can get down here.'

Bob Whitney made a remark that was favourably received by them all. 'Let's ride down there and visit the eatery . . . Bruce?'

Evans nodded and led off for their horses. The men from Battleboro weren't as hungry as Bruce and his companions were but they could eat.

Claude Garret was one of the first to get rigged out and mounted. He rested both hands on the saddle swells gazing in the direction of Barnum. Eventually he spat amber, reset his hat and addressed Bruce.

'That lawman's a mean old son of a bitch. I wouldn't bet you a plugged *centavo* he won't try to lock us all up.'

Nearby Al Hopper butted in. 'Feedin' an' carin' for the crew of us'll bankrupt his town. I'd as leave set in his jailhouse gettin' fed an' watered for a year. Rain and cold couldn't get me.'

Bruce looked mildly disgusted when he said, 'Let's go an' let's agree; we're not goin' down to bust Asa out nor pick any fights.'

A rider from Battleboro said in a subdued voice, 'We won't have to.'

The townsfolk saw them coming. The sun was high, the day was hot and the visibility was perfect.

Bruce adopted the same slow gait the sheriff had used earlier. He had no idea what a psychological advantage was but he had no trouble providing a leadership that favoured the animals.

He was riding Birch Tucker's compact, muscled-up Morgan horse with the wavy mane and heavy tail.

Despite the fact that the sheriff had said they were not to enter Barnum there was no one on the outskirts to stop or turn them back. No one commented, their total interest was on the eatery located on the east side of the road roughly mid-way among other business establishments. Its tie rack was not long enough to accommodate all their animals so the horses were tethered at nearby hitch racks.

There were people along the roadway watching them. Mostly they were like statues. There was no sign of the sheriff, his beefy big deputy or the riders who had accompanied them out to meet with the Battleboro men.

When they pushed past the door the caféman froze and a pair of elderly duffers who were eating from bowls of broth, got up, put coins beside half-empty bowls and left.

Walter Corrigan told Bob Whitney he'd eat anything that was hot and enough and went to stand at the roadway window.

People were gathering across from the eatery. He was unable to see if this was happening on the café's side too but assumed that it was.

It would have worried him more if it had been exclusively men but there were women and even a scattering of youngsters. Corrigan correctly assumed the gathering townsfolk were curious. Barnum had been on edge for several days. Its residents would have every right to be curious.

When the 'breed called, Corrigan left the window. The tantalizing aroma of cooked food made Corrigan and his companions attack their platters and coffee cups. It was not a question of quality it was a matter of quantity. But the food was substantial, abundant and flavourful.

The stone-faced caféman had no time for conversation, he was kept on the move. Eventually he put the huge old graniteware coffee pot on the counter.

His customers were beginning to slack off, to discreetly belch and relax when the sheriff's daughter walked in. This time without her Stetson hat.

The diners saw her but paid little heed, they were more concerned with eating and guzzling vast amounts of black java.

Bruce Evans twisted. She gave her

head a slight sideways gesture. He arose and followed her to a far corner of the room.

As he would learn in time she was a direct person as she demonstrated when she said, 'The sheriff sent me to talk to you.'

Bruce nodded without speaking.

'He will compromise.'

'What does that mean?'

'He'll release Taunton.'

'Lady, he's already said he'd do that. He's got no real reason for arresting him.'

She spoke as though there had been no interruption. 'He will send Asa Tucker to be held at the jailhouse up in Carlsbad, a hundred miles from Barnum until the circuit rider gets here.'

Bruce considered the woman. She was attractive without being pretty. Without that damned hat she looked feminine. He smiled at her. 'Ma'am, I'd like to tell you somethin'.'

'What?'

'If we'd come together under different circumstances I'd invite you buggy ridin'.'

Maryanne Holt's eyes widened. She hadn't anticipated anything personal. She avoided Bruce's gaze briefly before speaking again. This time her voice was crisp and businesslike. 'I think you should accept the sheriff's terms. You can have your rider; he'll make sure young Tucker is out of the reach of lynchers and all you have to do is go back where you came from.'

Bruce had no difficulty switching from the personal to the impersonal. 'Ma'am, if they want to lynch Asa their best chance would be when he was taken out of the jailhouse to be taken somewhere else. And, no, ma'am, we are not goin' back without him.' Bruce cocked his head slightly. 'I thought you was goin' to take his side. Right now you're sure not sounding like it.'

She looked straight at Bruce Evans. 'I am representing him. That's why I convinced the sheriff to get him out of Barnum. There's another reason, Mr Evans; I don't want a fight.'

'There won't be no fight, ma'am, if your pa'll just set Asa loose.'

'Mister Evans, do they have a telegraph where you came from?'

'No, ma'am.'

'There is one in Barnum.'

'Are you threatening me with soldiers, ma'am?'

'Not soldiers, US federal marshals. The sheriff telegraphed for them yesterday. Do you know what'll happen if you persist in being stubborn? They'll arrive with government authority to call in soldiers if they want to. Mister Evans, *go home*. Don't let this go any further . . . please.'

The diners had paid, left the counter to go outside for a smoke. They acted as though they did not see the woman or Bruce.

Because Bruce was silent she pushed her point. 'He'll have to stand trial. Nothing will change that. But you and your friends intimidating the town won't help your friend. Leave his protection to me.'

Bruce looked incredulous and she interpreted the look correctly. She said, 'It's not just me. Do you know who Bonner Watkins is?'

He shook his head although he had a notion that he might have heard the name before. She enlightened him.

'He's the partner of the man named Arnold young Tucker killed. They arrived here together. After the killing of Arnold he seemed to have disappeared.'

'That'd be a wise thing to do, ma'am.'

She had the appropriate answer to that. 'You can call outlaws clever, sly, dangerous, anything but wise. Bonner traded his worn-down saddle animal for a stout blue roan the day after Arnold was killed. He went west of here a day's ride and robbed a way-station where a stage was having its hitch changed and made off with a money box.'

'Ma'am, what's that got to do with Asa Tucker?'

Again her reply was put forth as though there had been no interruption. 'The blue roan lamed up on him. It had ring bones bad. He went to a religious community a few miles from where he had to leave the blue roan to steal another animal. Would you care to hear the rest of it, Mr Evans?'

He shrugged. He could tell from her expression he was going to be told whether he was interested or not and he was right, except that what she had to say halted him dead in his tracks.

'He'd holed up in a barn loft. He shot a man who caught him stealing a horse. Mister Evans, he's still in that loft.'

'How many folks are at that place, ma'am?'

'About thirty, mostly women, but with men too.'

'Why don't they smoke him out an' hang him?'

'Because it's against their faith to take a life.'

Bruce stood looking at her in long silence before speaking. 'He's still there?'

'Yes.'

'Do you know that place?'

'Better than that, Mr Evans, I know the people; I represented them against a land company back East who said they owned the land. I won.'

'Tell me how to get there, ma'am.'

'I'll do better, I'll take you there.'

Bruce's gaze drifted across the road to the jailhouse. Maryanne Holt made an accurate guess. 'Your friend will be safe. I know the sheriff. No one'll get inside his jailhouse and live to talk about it if he doesn't want them in there. He's my father.'

Bruce returned his gaze to the woman. 'It's his job to get this horse thief, not my job.'

'He can't do both jobs. Mister Evans, I need this Bonner Watkins to help me defend your friend.'

Bruce was thoughtful again for a long moment then bobbed his head. 'Get your horse, we'll wait for you at the north end of town.'

She corrected him. 'The south end, Mr Evans.'

He looked at her. 'Ma'am, I'd take it kindly if you'd quit callin' me Mr Evans. My name's Bruce.'

She shot back an answer. 'My name is Maryanne, not ma'am. I'll meet you at the lower end of town in fifteen minutes.'

He watched her cross the road and enter the jail-house, then left the café to tell the Battleboro men what she'd said.

Someone brought up the subject of Bonner Watkins being important and Bruce told them he might not be, but if he was the partner of the dead redhead, he might be valuable.

They seemed to accept that and went for their animals. The interested townsfolk were relieved to see them leave town, a few but not many recognized one rider who, although wearing a man's Stetson was a female woman.

Fortunately they got an early start, the men and their mounts were fresh. Under such circumstances it was possible to cover considerable land in excellent time.

Maryanne Holt said very little. Not even to Bruce Evans while riding stirrup with him.

7

The Herpetologist

There was an elegantly carved sign where the main coach road continued and a spur trail led mostly westerly but a little southerly. The sign said FOLLOWERS OF THE NEW LIGHT and beneath that in smaller letters were the words GOD'S PROMISE OF ETERNAL SALVATION.

The founder and head Indian, Maryanne told them, was a short, possum-bellied man named Alfred Newton. She described him well but for one omission, she didn't mention that Elder Newton, as he preferred to be called, was a glib spellbinder who, detractors said, suffered from verbal dysentery.

And they were right.

For some reason the men from

127

Battleboro never enquired about riders who turned off the coach road being notified by heliograph of their approach. When Bruce and his companions reached the extensive compound with its dozens of neat small cabins the Eternal Salvation Council was waiting on the long, covered porch of the meeting house, four in number ranging from a short individual wearing a white shawl with black embroidered lines at each end. He recognized the sheriff's daughter and raised his right hand palm forward in greeting. She returned the salute, led up and dismounted to introduce Bruce Evans and to ask if the horse thief was still in the loft.

He was and because he was one of God's creatures the followers of the brotherhood had supplied him with water and food.

He of 'the enlightened' with the rotund belly and white shawl told them, looking at Maryanne Holt as he spoke, that although they had offered

God's forgiveness for his being a horse-stealing son of a bitch he would not come down.

Bruce asked about the man who had been shot and Elder Newton made a dismissive gesture. 'He was buried yesterday.'

At the odd looks his attitude elicited among the rangemen Elder Newton explained. 'It is the wish for all sinners to be rinsed of their sins through the passing. He is now at the right hand of the Lord.'

Bruce turned to consider the barn. It, like all the structures, was solidly made, advantageously placed and expertly constructed.

He handed his reins to Bob Whitney and would have walked over there but Elder Newton said, 'He is in atonement. The longer he stays up there the more his guilt will increase.'

Rory Kildare asked how long he had been up there. The rotund, shawled man replied without hesitation. 'Two days and three nights.'

'You sure, mister, he didn't sneak out by now?'

'We are sure, brother. We've taken turns at vigilance from inside the barn. We've talked to him and he's spoken to us. We believe he is almost ready to yield.'

Rory Kildare coughed.

Bruce asked if it would be all right if he went to the barn to also talk to the renegade son of a bitch and Elder Newton said, 'We should eat first, Mr Evans. Allow him a few more hours for contrition to work.'

The 'breed rangeman abruptly sat on the ground and Elder Newton made the sign of the cross in his direction as he smiled and spoke.

'We newcomers to this land have only begun to appreciate the faith and rituals of its natives. They rely on their Great Spirit and while their system of obeisance differs from ours it is founded on identical convictions.'

The 'breed Al Hopper crossed his legs, tugged off one boot, emptied it

130

of a sharp bit of gravel, put the boot back on and stood up. Bruce and Bob Whitney exchanged a glance: so much for misinterpreting why the Indian had sat on the ground.

Elder Newton affected not to notice and was launching into a lengthy explanation of the philosophy of the faith of the new life when a man yelled from the barn.

'Brother Newton, I know who them bastards are. They got no right to be here an' I ain't comin' down but I'd sure admire bein' fed.'

The possum-bellied true believer spoke aside to a gaunt, sunken-eyed individual whose hairline came within three inches of his eyebrows and the gaunt man went inside the extensive room at his back.

Elder Newton showed his finest smile of indulgence. 'Do you know his name — the man in the loft?'

Bruce knew it. 'Bonner Watkins. He was the partner of a man named — '

'Yes, he told us; of an honest,

131

upstanding individual named Red Arnold who was murdered in the roadway of Barnum. Shot down in cold blood. We also knew from Brother Watkins the killer was locked in the Barnum jailhouse charged with murder.'

The gaunt man emerged behind his companions carrying two small tin buckets, ignored everyone as he passed through on his way to the barn.

A Battleboro man named Junior Roy spat amber, fixed his eyes on the man with the shawl and said, 'He killed one of your friends!'

Elder Newton used his indulgent smile during his reply. 'We are condemned to this life to pay for past sins. When we've properly repented and suffered, friend, we are taken to the Lord whose understanding and compassion are boundless. We don't weep over the dead, we exult in their passing.'

Junior Roy stared speechless. The man beside him gave Roy a nudge with his elbow.

A plain woman came out behind the

councilmen, spoke tersely and went back inside. She did not once look at the men standing with their horses.

Maryanne Holt knew these people; knew what was coming and spoke up. 'Elder Newton, we ate before leaving town. These men have come a long way and would like to return.'

'Miss Holt, a meal has been prepared. Our mealtimes are for anyone within sight.'

Bruce said, 'Mister, I'd like to talk with the feller in the loft. Maybe we can eat later.'

Elder Newton pointed. 'Leave your pistol here.'

Bruce handed the gun to Bob Whitney, walked in the direction of the barn, passed the gaunt man who did not look at Bruce and entered a barn where the fragrance of hay was strong. He saw the loft ladder and little else. He was addressed from somewhere beyond the place where the loft ladder ended. It was a square, fairly small opening called a 'crawl hole'.

The unseen speaker said, 'You try gettin' me, cowboy, and them folks'll be all over you like a rash.'

Bruce's reply was, 'Mister, from what I've heard they aren't violent folks. We're goin' to get you if we have to set down an' out-wait you.'

For a time the only sound from above was of someone eating. When that sound ended the invisible man said, 'First one of you pokes his head up that crawl hole will get eternal salvation, compliments of me.'

Bruce sought a seat, perched on the edge of a rickety saw horse and gazed out into dazzling daylight. Eventually he said, 'Your name's Bonner Watkins.'

'That's more'n I know about you except that you rode in here on a Morgan horse I've seen before.'

'That's why I'm here. That's the horse you'n your dead friend shot a friend of mine off an' left for dead, then sold the horse in Battleboro.'

'Good animal. I tried to talk Red

into lettin' me have him. He said as broke as we was he had to sell the horse. Red was usually right.'

'But not real smart. Mister Watkins, you two shouldn't have stopped in the place where we ship cattle.'

Bonner Watkins made drinking sounds and deliberately dropped the water bottle through the crawl hole as he said, 'Go home, cowboy. I'll set up here safe until next winter. These folks is real hospitable. Did they tell you how grateful they was for me shootin' that son of a bitch who caught me fixin' to steal one of their horses?'

Bruce responded as though there had been no question from above. 'Mister, come down out of there. You got until sundown. Then we'll burn the barn with you in it.'

Bonner Watkins loudly snorted. 'They'd cut you off at the water-line.'

'They don't believe in violence. If they did they'd have crawled up there and shot you.'

Bonner Watkins was briefly silent

before speaking again. 'You from that place where we sold the Morgan horse?'

'From thereabouts.'

'Go back, cowboy. I ain't comin' down an' I can wait you out if it takes a year. These is real hospitable folks.'

Bruce arose and was walking toward the door as he said, 'You better be fireproof, Brother Watkins.'

During his absence his companions had been subjected to a harangue about the pureness of the eternal salvation philosophy and watched Bruce crossing toward them from the barn. He was also being watched by the man in the loft who had cracked the mow door several inches. He was grinning.

When Bruce returned, the overstuffed man wearing the shawl paused in his sermon to ask what luck Evans had had.

'None,' he answered. 'Brother, there's a way of getting him down out of there. Burn your barn down.'

Elder Newton and his silent elders

stared. One of them said, 'Mister, we was three years building that barn. The Lord would visit on them as sought to destroy it.'

Bruce turned, led his companions to the barn where their animals could be watered and fed and the man who had said the Lord would bring vengeance addressed Elder Newton.

'We can't let them do that.'

Elder Newton nodded. 'It won't happen. When we prayed for the logs and all He provided them. He did as much as any of us. That's His barn as much as it's our barn.'

The anxious council member had a question. 'You're plumb right, Elder. He sweated right along with us. Now why has He put that imp of Satan in our loft an' brought those fellers who want to burn the barn to get the bastard out?'

'Brother, you know as well as the rest of us that the Lord works in mysterious ways.'

'They're mysterious for a fact, Elder,

but I got to say since He went an' made us His chosen on earth why don't He give me some relief for ruinin' my back gettin' those logs in place for His barn?'

The complainer's peevishness was ignored as Elder Newton said they should all go inside and eat. Whether the others had observed it or not his uniqueness included an ability to pray with a mouthful of food.

At the barn there was little talk and none from the loft until the sheriff's daughter went to stand below the crawl hole and say, 'Why did you let your drunk partner go out into the roadway where he got killed?'

The answer stopped movement down below. 'Red warn't all that drunk. We was partners several years. I seen him like he was that afternoon many times. He'd go out, I'd go out too, take a place in a recessed doorway an' shoot first. It always worked.'

'Not this time,' the woman said.

'Lady, me'n Red been at the outlawin'

business a long time. Up until this time mostly up north near the Canadian line where we got two caches.'

Before Maryanne Holt could speak again, Bruce said, 'You rode in the wrong direction. Montana is north not south-west.'

Bonner Watkins sounded almost contemptuous when he replied, 'The damned horse I stole in Barnum lamed up. I found this place. With a sound animal under me I figured to go far out an' around, then head north.'

Bob Whitney said, 'You let your partner get killed?'

'It was time to quit. Red was gettin' harder to get along with, gettin' meaner'n meaner.'

Nothing more was said, not even after the men trooped outside in the midday heat, but several of them wagged their heads, perfectly willing to thank Elder Newton's God there weren't too many Bonner Watkinses in the world.

Bruce saw the men emerging from

the long building, Elder Newton in the lead. There were more men, about twenty-five of them. They ignored the men down at the barn, followed Newton to the only stone structure in the compound and went inside. It was time for prayer. Followers Of The New Light prayed four times a day. In summertime they lingered to pray longest. Stone buildings were blessedly cool, ideal structures to find escape from the heat.

There was impatience. Rory Kildare said they had Watkins where he couldn't escape, so what in hell were they waiting for? Bob Whitney answered dryly, 'Waitin' for someone to climb up that ladder. You care for the job, Rory?'

The Battleboro saloonman did not speak. Neither did any of the others. For a plain and obvious fact that was what had to be done but how to do it without getting shot was something else.

Maryanne Holt had an idea. 'Give

him an animal and let him run for it. We can chase him down if it takes a week.'

Several of the men looked disgusted but said nothing. One of the brotherhood came to the barn. He was youngish with soft features and a palpable innocence. His name didn't matter but it was Abel Richman. He was pleasant in an abstract way and was not interested in the outlaw above. He told them he was a herpetologist and smiled at Bruce who didn't smile back while he tried to imagine what a herpetologist was. The gentle brother explained.

'I collect snakes. All kinds. I got a rocked-up place where I'm allowed to keep them. I got some pretty ones. None of the folks care for my snakes but I do.'

The 'breed said, 'You make pets of snakes?'

'Not exactly. Gopher an' grass snakes'll let me handle them, play with them but sidewinders an' rock rattlers don't like me.'

The men and Maryanne considered the pleasant, guileless face. Maryanne asked him a question. 'How do you catch them?'

'With a draw string at the end of a pole. Get it over their heads. Some slide into rocks where I can't get 'em but rattlesnakes don't run from me. They coil and get set to strike with their heads up. They're the easiest to catch. I got about nine of 'em. I can show you. It's not far. Elder Newton don't want them close to the yard. He worried they'll get loose. But I rocked 'em in so they can't get loose.'

Practical Walter Corrigan asked the younger man how he fed them and got a quiet reply. 'It keeps me busy poking around under rocks and deadfalls. They eat . . . that's why I stopped catching them. They eat all I can get. Sometimes in bad weather I get kitchen scraps. They eat big then go into the rocks and sleep. I guess that's what they do. Some are friendly and some aren't. I'd like to show them to you folks. The brothers don't go see them. They mostly got no use for snakes. I think some of 'em are real pretty. Want me to show you?'

Maryanne led off, Bruce followed her, several others trooped along but most of the men lingered at the barn, not especially afraid but not especially interested in what they thought was a simpleton's peculiar hobby.

Snakes give off a peculiar faint smell, especially when they are moulting and acquiring new skins. Any confined reptiles gave their confined area a unique aroma.

The guileless collector of snakes was pleased. Among his associates no one liked his hobby nor visited the carefully rocked-up area of confinement. When they reached it, their guide said in order to prevent his pets from burrowing out he'd had to make a base of solid rock two feet deep and it had taken him nearly all summer to do it.

'That,' Maryanne told Bruce quietly, 'is dedication.'

Sunning snakes disappeared among

the rocks at sight of the youth and his companions. Several went into a menacing coil.

Their keeper smiled broadly. 'That one with the dark head's got no rattles. They must've got caught in some rocks. He'll grow new ones in a year or so but he can't grow no five or six rattles for a long time.'

The 'breed who'd had skirmishes with rattlesnakes many times made an obvious statement. 'That one you'd ought to kill. He can't rattle to warn folks. Someday someone'll step up too close . . .'

Richman looked at the 'breed. 'Him and me is getting close to being friends. He don't know he can't rattle. Some days I find mice and after he eats he hides for two, three days. I call him Seneca after an In'ian in a book my pa used to read to me. Seneca don't make any noise. He could slip right up to folks. He's getting tame . . . watch.'

There was no gate into the compound but the wall of stones surrounding it had been fitted and filled so perfectly Richman's pets couldn't get out and since reptiles are not good climbers his wall did not have to be more than about three feet high.

Richman climbed over in a worn place he used often. Snakes silently glided for cover, except for three rattlers. They went into their defensive coil and made their tails quiver. The rattler named Seneca did everything his companions did, made his tail quiver without any sound accompanying the quivering.

Richman moved confidently and slowly. One snake abruptly came out of his coil and glided rapidly to a place of concealment in some rocks.

One snake's tail quivered fiercely as it raised its head, weaving slightly from left to right, forked tongue flickering rapidly in and out.

Abel Richman groped in a trouser pocket, drew forth a dead mouse, very slowly knelt, put the mouse on the ground and eased it toward the tailless rattlesnake with the toe of one boot.

Bob Whitney addressed none of the motionless watchers when he softly said, 'Crazy as a pet 'coon.'

That was the only comment as Richman moved back slowly and squatted. It was not as long a wait as it had been but the tailless rattler eventually lowered his head, small, lidless black eyes moving from the squatter to the mouse.

Richman spoke quietly. 'He hasn't eaten good in four, five days.'

Seneca's coils loosened, he eased his flat head from side to side and toward the mouse, halting occasionally to stare at Richman. Once when he did this Richman spoke softly to him and that caused an even longer motionless stillness. Al Hopper sat down, his companions remained standing.

Seneca glided cautiously. No matter how many mice his owner had fed him, Seneca was still wild and wary. He took a long time to get poised to grab the mouse but he eventually did it and had to raise his head higher, jaws sprung, to swallow the mouse.

The guileless herpetologist arose very slowly and made a remark that switched attention from the snake to Richman. In his quiet voice he said, 'All you got to do if you want that feller down from the loft is wait until it's dark enough, then climb up there and toss Seneca in there.'

The men and Maryanne Holt were still and silent until she said, 'Can you catch other rattlers, ones with tails that make noise?'

Richman pointed to a lengthy staff with a slip knot at the far end and loosely confining keepers made of discarded tin cans at spaced intervals from the slipknot end to a large knot at the other end which kept the cotton cord in place.

'You don't want Seneca?' he asked.

Maryanne shook her head. 'Noisy ones. Can you catch four or five?'

'Yes'm,' the youth said and went to

pick up his snake rod and a dirty old croaker sack.

He was careful and persistent. It took more than an hour to catch and sack three wrist-thick rattlers, one of them a prime diamond back. He put up the hardest fight.

Bruce told Maryanne three should be enough.

On the walk back to the yard the youth gave them a graphic re-enactment of how he had used half a day to snare that stubby diamond back.

They believed him. As they were entering the barn from the rear, that cadaverous man was descending the ladder with empty small pots which had contained Bonner Watkins' supper.

It wasn't until then Maryanne and her companions realized how much time they had spent with the herpetologist.

In its furtive way dusk was approaching.

8

The Pepperbox

A large muscular man with unruly light hair came to the barn to say supper was ready, which was probably true but the large man fooled no one, his gaze probed in all directions. When he saw Abel Richman he said, 'You'd better come with me. Elder Newton needs you up in the kitchen.'

The Battleboro men closed up in front of the croaker sack with its snakes which had room to coil and would not rattle until they had space.

Abel Richman left the barn with the large man. He neither spoke nor looked left or right. Elder Newton evidently understood the persuasive power of force.

The 'breed favoured going over yonder and getting something to eat. Bruce

Evans, conscious of the possibility that the outlaw in the loft heard everything said, nodded. Maryanne and the others followed Bruce out of the barn. He halted part way and said eating could wait, they should split up, half to re-enter the barn from out back, half to return by the front entrance and not to make a sound.

There was no discussion, the rangemen wearing spurs knelt to remove them. Bruce led off toward the barn's front opening.

It was darker inside the barn than it was outside. The only light came from the large building where the cultists were eating.

If Bonner Watkins heard anything he gave no sign of it, but he would be up there, fed, comfortable, confident and safe.

Bruce gestured for the 'breed to shed his boots. While this was being done Bob Whitney brought the sack over.

The 'breed stood up, studied the

loft ladder, took the sack and shook it. The snakes reacted to being jostled. The 'breed looked at his companions and grinned, moved to the ladder and with one hand holding rungs began a slow and careful ascent.

Down below several men palmed handguns.

When the 'breed was close enough to reach for the final rung Bruce Evans called to the outlaw.

'You asleep up there?'

Watkins answered curtly. 'Come up an' see.'

Evans said, 'Don't make so much damned noise. I got a proposition for you.'

'There's nothin' you got I want,' the outlaw replied.

'Shut up an' listen. While everyone's over yonder eatin' I'll rig out a horse. You get on it an' light out. I'll catch up. We'll go find them caches an' split.'

This time the horse thief was longer replying. 'What's your name?'

'Bruce Evans.'

'Evans, you think I come down in the last rain? You got to do better'n that.'

Al Hopper, the 'breed, was holding the last rung in his left hand. He was crouching as he rolled back as much of the sack as he could manage to do one-handed. When he was ready he bobbed his head.

Bruce called again. 'All right; I'll rig out a horse an' go over yonder until I hear you runnin' for it, then I'll go lookin' for you.'

Bonner Watkins sourly said, 'Sure you will, with all them rangemen along with you.'

Hopper raised his head above the opening, hurled the sack and descended by using both hands and not touching rungs with his feet.

He hadn't quite reached the floor when the outlaw let out a shout, loud as it was it did not drown out rattlesnakes quivering their tails.

Bonner Watkins swore in an agitated

voice. He called Bruce every name he could think of.

The rattling continued, whether Watkins could see the snakes or not he could hear them. Neither Bonner Watkins or the waiting men below knew whether snakes could see in the dark. They couldn't; their eyesight was very good in daylight, but three angry large snakes rattling was enough.

Bonner Watkins swore and moved at the same time. The 'breed called up to him. 'There's five of 'em. You step on one an' mister . . . '

The loft inhabitant cursed again. When he went silent Elder Newton and two of his brothers walked in. One of the brothers was carrying a lantern. Walter Corrigan wrenched it away and blew down the mantle. The man he'd snatched the lantern from growled and lunged. Corrigan was holding the lamp. Two rangemen came in from both sides and struck the angry man. From above, Bonner Watkins called derisively, 'Sure you'd help me escape, Mr Evans, you lyin' son of a bitch . . . Elder? You down there?'

Newton answered from just inside the wide front barn opening. 'I'm here, brother.'

'Get them bastards out'n here or I'll start shootin'.'

Elder Newton helped his companion the lantern-bearer to his feet. The man who had been knocked down evidently had retained something of his former life; he lacked the humility of his fellow cultists. He shook loose and faced the nearest rangeman, who was Bob Whitney.

'Shed that pistol, mister,' he snarled. 'An' I'll clean your plough.'

Elder Newton made a clucking sound of disapproval which had no effect on his angry follower who glared. 'One at a time, you sons of bitches, an' I'll break your damned bones.'

This time Elder Newton looked shocked but only those closest to him could see that. He brushed the angry man's arm. 'Leave it be, Brother

154

Harold. Just leave it be.'

From the loft came a bitter laugh followed by a statement from Bonner Watkins. 'Run 'em off, Elder. Disarm 'em an' run 'em off.'

Maryanne who had remained in dark shadows up until now called to the outlaw, 'I'm the sheriff's daughter. Come down and I'll promise you you won't be hurt.'

This time the overhead voice dripped scorn. 'The sheriff's daughter, my butt. What in hell are you doin' with them . . . *snake! Fer Chris'sake I stepped on a snake!*'

There was no mistaking the fear in the outlaw's outcry.

Al Hopper laughed. No one else did. Hopper called upwards. 'You got high top boots, mister? He can't strike no higher'n he can raise his head.'

Bonner Watkins's next shout drowned out half of what Hopper had said, 'I'm comin' down. Get out'n the way.'

Watkins came through the loft hole groping for the ladder. He didn't turn to descend in the normal way, he came down face forward and missed half the rungs.

Walter Corrigan was closest. He caught the outlaw with his left hand and hit him hard with his right hand.

Bonner Watkins fell in a heap.

Elder Newton started forward, ostensibly to help. The 'breed cocked his fist and Elder Newton stopped.

Maryanne came from dark shadows to pluck the six-gun from the unconscious man's holster. She handed it to Bruce and stepped aside as the 'breed and Walter Corrigan dragged the outlaw out of the barn where starshine showed a trickle of blood at one corner of the mouth of Bonner Watkins.

The 'breed stood over the outlaw. The gentle-faced snake owner brushed past to climb into the loft.

Maryanne stopped him. 'Wait for daylight. They wouldn't know it's you. We'll help you catch them come daylight.'

The youth smiled at Maryanne and

did not approach the ladder. Several rangemen rolled their eyes. No one with good sense would try to corral upset rattlers in broad daylight let alone in a dark barn loft.

Elder Newton turned to leave with his fiery-tempered companion. Bruce went after him; he needed a place where the captive could be chained until morning. Elder Newton spoke to his companion and continued on in the direction of the large lighted community building.

The man who had been knocked down considered Bruce without moving or speaking until the 'breed, Bob Whitney and two other rangemen came out of the barn and grabbed the groggy horse thief. He turned and led the way to a small, massive log structure where he took some chains from a wall and threw them at Bruce Evans's feet.

He did not say a word. He left the rangemen, heading for the lighted large building.

Bonner Watkins was chained to

a wall. He was aware but he'd taken a powerful blow. He considered his captors. 'Gawddamned rattlesnakes. I've seen how fellers got bit by them slimy varmints . . . How'd you get 'em up there?'

No one provided an answer. The 'breed ignored the prisoner. He was still hungry and said so.

It was chilly; cold was the precursor of dawn. This was another time when the passage of time had been ignored.

Walter Corrigan did not think it was a sound idea to leave their prisoner alone but relented with a shrug when none of the hungry men volunteered to keep watch.

They trooped over to the lighted building and were met in the doorway by the man who had been knocked down. He hesitated just long enough before letting them enter to glare at Bob Whitney.

There was no sign of Elder Newton; there wouldn't be for several hours; he was not a particular eater, he was one of those people who valued quantity over quality.

There were several women and a few men clearing a long table. In the adjoining kitchen there were only women.

Bruce Evans was about to mention being fed when that hot-tempered brother, whom Whitney had struck, fixed Evans with a smouldering look and grudgingly pointed to chairs. 'Set,' he said and disappeared in the kitchen.

One of the women, an arrow-straight individual with a lipless wound of a mouth and cold dark eyes, would have taken the sheriff's daughter into the kitchen to be fed separately from the beard-stubbled, unwashed-looking men but Maryanne shook her head, took a chair at the table between a rangeman with a prominent Adam's apple, and Hopper.

As happens, hunger as a motivating force was undeniable but what it became once food was available was something related to starvation. No one talked, they ate and when a platter was emptied a cult woman refilled it, rolled her eyes and went back and forth for close to an hour before the diners began to ease up.

Walter Corrigan left the house to look in on the prisoner. Why he should be uneasy was anyone's guess. When he opened the door and met the sullen gaze of Bonner Watkins he was relieved.

The prisoner said, 'How much money would it take for you to turn me loose?'

Corrigan replied curtly, which was his manner. 'You don't have that much.'

Watkins showed a crafty grin. 'Let's start at a thousand dollars an' go up from there.' Because Walter Corrigan's expression of dislike remained fixed, the outlaw tried again. 'You're a real joker, ain't you? Name a figure, friend. There's caches up north.'

Corrigan's expression did not change. 'An' you'n me would find a cache an' split . . . Mister, I been around my share of sons of bitches like you. You'd lie when the truth'd fit better.'

Corrigan returned to the long room and nodded when men looked enquiringly at him. He then resumed his place at the table and went to work on whatever serving platters still had food on them.

Daylight was close. Bruce Evans went to the kitchen door to thank the women. They ignored him completely so he dropped his hat on and followed the others out into newday cold.

They would need a horse, Bonner Watkins had arrived without one. Bruce went looking for Elder Newton, found his log house which was not unlike the others except that it was situated a right smart distance away in a stand of trees with a pole fence to assure privacy. The only reason for fences in livestock open range country was to prevent loose cattle from ruining orchards and demolishing painstakingly cultivated flower and vegetable plantings. Since the cult appeared not to have any livestock it was left to wonder why the Paramount Elder needed such privacy.

They were never to know why, but it could have had something to do with a dented scrap of copper tubing lying in grass where it had been discarded. Although it was customary for religious folks to abhor alcoholic beverages copper tubing was an essential necessity of a whiskey still.

A rawboned woman whose greying hair was pulled strictly back on both sides of her head met them at the door with a flinty expression. When they asked to see Elder Newton they were told in hard, clipped words that the Elder was in meditation and could not be disturbed. She then wanted to know their reason for audience and when Bruce told her they needed to borrow a horse for their prisoner she said, 'Maryanne Holt's horse carries double,' and closed the door.

Maryanne nodded at Bruce without

speaking until they were out of the fenced-in compound, then she agreed that her animal was broke to carry double and also said, 'That's Sister Elmira, Elder Newton's housekeeper. She's been that since his wife died four years ago.'

The men from Battleboro were inclined to accept that on the visible grounds that Sister Elmira was plumb without any of the female attractions necessary for Elder Newton or any other man to keep her around for other purposes.

When they got to the barn with Bonner Watkins he raised the same question and Maryanne Holt gave him the same answer. It was clear in the outlaw's expression that riding behind someone's cantle lacked a lot of being his idea of comfortable transportation but he said nothing beyond leaning to scratch his lower shank near the top of his right boot.

The horses were up in the bit; their riders may not have achieved a period of rest but the horses had. Also, as with their riders, they had full stomachs.

When they rigged out, got astride with Maryanne carrying Bonner Watkins behind her saddle, they rode out of the yard without a single member or follower of The New Light brotherhood in sight among the buildings or in the yard.

A rangeman with looped reins so he could build a smoke using both hands licked the wheat-straw paper, closed it and was preparing to light up when he said, 'Why'n we hang this son of a bitch out here somewhere?'

There was a delay before he got an answer. 'Because we need him to explain to the sheriff how Birch's brother wasn't supposed to kill Red Arnold. He was supposed to be baited out into the roadway to face Asa an' Bonner Watkins was to shoot first an' kill Asa from a hidin' place. Sheriff Holt's got to be told it was murder by accident. This smelly, weasel-faced son of a bitch was part of somethin' him an' Red Arnold had done before.'

Bruce twisted to look at the prisoner. Bonner Watkins looked straight back. Maryanne sitting in front of the outlaw was erect and expressionless in the saddle.

Bonner Watkins said, 'That's about how it worked. That young buck wouldn't have had a chance except that I didn't kill him. I let him kill Red.'

No one spoke for a fair distance, then it was Bonner Watkins. Without raising his voice he said, 'You gents can't see it but I got a pepperbox against her back above the bead of the cantle.' Watkins paused for reaction. There was none, the horses continued to move, their riders sat slightly more erect in their saddles and Bruce Evans eased up to drift back. Bonner Watkins said, 'Stay where you are. Don't none of you get clever. I'd as leave blow her innards out past her belt buckle as suck air . . . One at a time, gents, drop your handguns.' When there was delay Watkins spoke again and this

165

time although he did not raise his voice there was no mistaking its harshness. '*Do it!*'

Maryanne's face was white to the front brim of her hat. Bob Whitney dropped his belt-gun. Two other riders followed his example. The 'breed was the last rider to disarm himself. He, with several others still had booted Winchesters.

Bonner Watkins told them to shed the carbines and this time although the 'breed obeyed, his reluctance was obvious. He said, 'I'm goin' to lift your hair!'

Bonner Watkins considered Al Hopper. 'Say somethin' like that again, you mongrel bastard, an' I'll kill you.'

The 'breed was silent and remained silent but his dark glare spoke volumes.

'Now then,' Watkins said in that harsh tone, 'Get off them horses.'

Bruce addressed the sheriff's daughter. 'Is he tellin' the truth? Has he got a pistol in your back?'

Because she didn't trust herself to

speak Maryanne nodded.

Walter Corrigan let his reins hang loose. As his mount began slackening Bonner Watkins said, 'I told you, act clever an' I'll kill you. Keep that horse up with the others. *Get off them horses!*'

That was Bonner Watkins's first mistake. As the men halted and swung down, one man, the 'breed Indian, hurled something from the far side of his mount. Impact knocked Bonner Watkins forward. When his head struck Maryanne she twisted and struck hard. Watkins fell. Before he could arise the 'breed was above him. He picked up the pepperbox pistol and threw it as far as he could. He then yanked the outlaw to his feet and punched toward Maryanne as he said, 'Get up there! Next time I'll cut your lousy throat. *Get up there!*'

Two unsmiling rangemen, one on each side, rode with Maryanne as the ride was resumed.

Walter Corrigan asked the 'breed

what he'd hit Watkins with and Hopper held up a stone-handled boot knife. 'I never could make one stick. The stone handle hit him in the back of the neck. We'd ought to shoot the son of a bitch.'

Corrigan made one of his terse statements. 'Not yet. Not until he tells his story to the sheriff.'

9

Dust and Sweat

Before they had Barnum in sight they could hear a train letting off steam. By the time the buildings were in view the departing train made enough noise to drown out all other sound.

Maryanne led them up a back alley on the west side of town. She drew rein and dismounted behind the jailhouse, looped her reins and went up to the rear door where she knocked.

There was no immediate response. She knocked harder the second time and when the door swung inward the sheriff was holding a shotgun. At sight of his daughter and the rangemen he lowered the gun, stepped aside for her to enter and would have slammed the door when she stopped him.

'They can come in. It's a long story.'

She shouldered past her father and gestured for the stockmen to come inside, which they did after making their animals fast along a dilapidated wooden fence.

Sheriff Holt stood like a statue. When they shoved Bonner Watkins in the sheriff said, 'Who's this one?'

He got no reply until they were all in the jailhouse office, then his daughter sat down, thumbed back her hat and began talking.

There was a hanging *olla*. One thirsty individual took it down and drank. He established a precedent. Other rangemen crowded up, drank until the *olla* was empty then sat loosely on a long wall bench and three rickety chairs.

When Maryanne stopped talking her father went to a wall rack, put the shotgun in its niche, crossed to his desk and sat down.

He said, 'You're Watkins, the other feller's partner?'

Bonner nodded without speaking.

'You say my daughter told the truth?'

Bonner Watkins was uncomfortable enough to cross and recross his legs before nodding again, except that this time he also spoke.

'That's pretty much the way things happened, except for that possum-bellied saint, or whatever he is, said if the law hunted me down him'n his partners wouldn't let 'em get at me.'

Sheriff Holt dismissed this with a scowl. 'You'n your partner baited that young feller out into the roadway? You done that other times?'

'Sheriff, this ain't a nice world. Fellers got to survive any way they can.'

The sheriff glared. 'Folks like you don't make it any better. You'n that redheaded feller.' Holt paused. 'You was goin' to shoot that boy in the back?'

'Not exactly, Sheriff. If that bronco hadn't got his ruff up. We done what we had to do. We wasn't neither one of us real fast with a gun.'

Bruce interrupted. 'Like catchin' a lone rider out a ways an' shootin' him for his horse?'

'Like I said, keepin' body an' soul together folks got to do whatever is necessary.'

'Murder? For a horse?'

'Sheriff, you know much about horses? I do. My pa raised 'em an' sold 'em to the Army, traded all over hell in a wagon with his tradin' stock tied to the tailgate until I was big enough to do the herdin'. My pa knew horses better'n any man alive. I learnt from him. Me'n Red was in strange country, damn near broke. I seen that feller up ahead a piece. I told Red what we'd do an' he asked what in hell was so important of doin' it this close to a town.'

'I told him that there was a Morgan horse. He'd bring top dollar.'

'So you shot the feller ridin' him?'

Bonner nodded, drifted his gaze to Maryanne where it briefly lingered before moving to Bruce Evans. 'How'd you get them snakes into the loft?'

Bruce answered dryly. 'Put 'em in a sack an' tossed 'em up there.'

'You had a sack of rattlesnakes with you?'

Bruce didn't believe this question required an answer so he gave none. He looked from the sheriff to his daughter. 'I'd sure admire to see them boys of ours you got locked up, Mr Holt.'

The answer could have been anticipated but it wasn't. The sheriff said, 'So would a dozen men around town. They aren't goin' to, mister, an' neither are you.' The lawman paused before continuing, 'If there was a way I could give 'em to you I would do it. That lanky one named Alamo something-or-other . . . I never saw a man as could eat like he does. I've owned cows that couldn't hold a candle to him. Mister Evans, you ever consider wormin' him?'

Maryanne changed the subject and her father frowned when she said, 'Asa

Tucker killed that redheaded man in self-defence.'

Her father exploded. 'Self-defence! I still want to hear more on this, so does most of Barnum. Maryanne, half the town saw that young buck brace the redheaded stranger in the middle of the road. How do you make self-defence out of that!'

'It was a set-up, like I told you, like Watkins told you himself. The redheaded one deliberately allowed himself to be called outside. Bonner Watkins slipped out, got into a recessed doorway and figured to fire first — at my client. That would have been murder. My client got baited pure and simple. He defended himself.'

'Is that a fact? Maryanne, Asa Tucker called the redheaded man. He figured to shoot him an' he was too drunk to draw.'

'Not too drunk, Pa. He knew he wouldn't have to draw. Just walk out there and let Bonner Watkins murder him. He already admitted all this!'

Sheriff Holt drummed on his desk top. After a moment he said, 'It'll be up to the circuit rider. My job is to lock 'em up. His job is to try 'em an' sentence 'em.'

Maryanne did not dispute this, she said, 'All my life you've told me a body has a right to defend himself. That's what Asa Tucker was doing.'

'Maryanne, Asa Tucker didn't know this here feller was to shoot first.'

She smiled at her father. 'That's my point, Pa. The one named Red Arnold and that feller yonder have done this before. They meant to kill my client. He didn't know it but they knew it. They baited him, he went into the roadway and Bonner Watkins was already in place to shoot first. All my client did was protect himself. You told me a hundred times folks — '

'Maryanne, let's let the judge sort this out.'

She nodded. 'I'm agreeable. Release my client on bail. Only the Lord knows when the judge'll get back to Barnum.'

'You know right well there's no bail for murder.'

This time she wasn't smiling as she spoke, 'Pa, it wasn't murder! It was self-defence.'

'No it warn't, girl. The dead one didn't even reach for his gun. He was too drunk to — '

'He didn't reach for it, Pa, because he knew he didn't have to. He was going to stand there and watch my client get shot from ambush.'

Bonner Watkins cleared his throat which made a distraction, Sheriff Holt glowered at him. 'If you was supposed to shoot first why didn't you?'

An answer would implicate cached loot up north. Bonner tried lying, something he'd developed into an art form through a lifetime of practice. 'My gun jammed, besides I couldn't get a sure shot from the doorway. They was facin' each other. Red was part way blockin' a clear shot.'

Walter Corrigan and Bruce Evans looked long and hard at the outlaw.

He fidgeted and cleared his throat again before weakly saying, 'It warn't a decent thing to do, set up a person an kill 'em from ambush.'

That was too much even for the sheriff. 'You set right there an' told us you did this other times.'

Someone rattled the jailhouse doorway with the barrel of a weapon.

Sheriff Holt jerked his head for someone else to open the door and without haste drew his leathered Colt and was holding it in his hand when the door was opened. The intruder was also holding a gun, his was hanging loose at one side and Holt's weapon was pointed with a thumb pad atop the hammer.

The intruder looked around, seemed surprised to find the room full and wagged his head. 'There's a committee,' he told the sheriff. 'Bud's over yonder with the others. He's tryin' to talk 'em down.' The intruder, obviously a townsman rather than a rangeman, was tall, ruddy-faced and for the moment clearly uncomfortable under the steady gaze of Bruce, the stone-faced 'breed and others.

He looked at Maryanne. 'This ain't somethin' a woman'd ought to be mixed up with.'

She almost ruefully smiled. 'Nothing of late is something for a woman to be involved with.' She knew the lanky townsman. 'Lester, what'd you expect to do with that gun?'

The townsman looked down, raised his right hand slowly and holstered the weapon. He was red in the face. Whatever his purpose for being at the jailhouse, he was obviously a fish out of water. In fact he was a harness-maker. He and Sheriff Holt had an ongoing Draughts session in which half the town had an interest. They were friends and that made the harnessmaker's reason for being there even more unpleasant.

He said, 'Will, you don't need that gun.'

The sheriff made no move to holster it as he said, 'Any time someone comes knockin' on my door with a gun barrel

I figure it's not a friendly call . . . Les, spit it out. What are you here for?'

'Will, that young buck did a murder with folks watchin'.'

The sheriff leathered his gun and leaned with both hands clasped atop his table. 'What do you want!'

'I represent a comitatus committee, Sheriff.'

'What is a comitatus committee?'

'It's sort of like a posse. I never heard of it before, neither.'

Maryanne's patience was exhausted. She knew what the term meant. She said, 'How many, Les?'

'Nine. They come down to my shop.'

'You make ten?'

'Yes'm.'

Maryanne faced her father. 'It's a group of lynchers.'

Sheriff Holt fixed the harness-maker with a withering look. 'They sent you? Why didn't they all come? Les, you tell your committee if I so much as see 'em across the road I'm goin' to start shootin'. You understand?'

The leather worker looked around the crowded room one more time and seemed about to speak when Sheriff Holt said, 'You tell my deputy to get his butt up here, *pronto*. Give me their names.'

'Can't do that, Will. I took an oath. That way they said after the hangin' folks wouldn't know who-all done it.'

Bonner Watkins spoke. 'Mister, you tell your friends the plan was to bushwhack that young feller. The feller he killed was the bait.'

After the harness-maker's departure Bob Whitney rolled his eyes. The sheriff saw this and said, 'He's real good workin' leather. His name's Lester Moody. He was born with one foot out of the stirrup. Friendly, decent, but with a few bricks shy of a load.'

Someone with the voice of a bull began roaring from the cell room. The Battleboro men recognized the voice. Alamo Taunton belonged to it.

The words were not altogether distinguishable but Taunton's friends

and companions had no trouble understanding that he was very upset over not
being fed.

Bob Whitney volunteered to cross
over to the eatery but Sheriff Holt
objected. He knew his town and its
inhabitants. There were more than
nine hot-heads. He suggested that
the upset rangemen could wait and
got arguments.

Maryanne broke the impasse. She
said she would go and also said she
too was hungry. It was a common
affliction, but the proposal by a female
woman struck them mute.

Her father arose, reset his hat and
without a word crossed to the door and
closed it after himself.

The rangemen crowded at the solitary
little barred roadway window. Not a
word was said as they watched the
lawman until Maryanne nudged Bruce
and jerked her head southward.

There was a band of men standing
motionless out front of the saddle and
harness shop. They were armed, at

least one man had a short-barrelled saddle gun in the crook of an arm.

Al Hopper snorted. He shared with many rangemen a tolerant contempt for townsmen.

The sheriff disappeared inside the eatery about the same time Alamo Taunton began bellowing again. Walter Corrigan reached for the ring of keys on a peg and headed for the cell room, Corrigan was not only a taciturn individual, he was a person in whom the difference between right and wrong were immutable.

No one made a move to interfere as lank Alamo Taunton and Asa Tucker left their cells in total silence, followed Corrigan to the jailhouse office and went to rummage the sheriff's drawers for their sidearms.

Without raising her voice, Maryanne said, 'You're going to make it worse,' and was ignored as Bruce went through a small, musty storeroom to open the back alley door and peer out. When he turned he spoke over his shoulder.

'Clear all the way to the livery barn.'

When Maryanne would have protested again, Bruce said, 'You better come with us.'

'Why?'

'Because they aren't goin' to believe you figured what we're doin' is right.'

She gazed impassively at Bruce while the men went into the little storeroom. Bruce was the last to go and looked at her, without speaking or moving until someone hissed irritably for Bruce to come along.

She seemed about to follow but didn't. Bruce hurried to catch up with the others. Bruce was correct, the alley was empty. In a town the size of Barnum there were dogs.

Wherever they were now wasn't in the alley. Not even at the livery barn where it was always cool with troughs of water.

The liveryman had been dozing in a tipped-back chair out front of his harness room when they entered and without speaking split into two groups, one to get horses the other group to get bridles, blankets and saddles. When he was awakened he was too stunned at the bustling activity to lean forward or speak, which was just as well. If he had been troublesome he would have been put down. There was no time for conversation.

Asa found the Morgan horse in a dingy stall dozing and led him out to be saddled by the men.

These were men who had been rigging out mounts since childhood. There was no waste motion. When they were ready a rough, faded man went up to the roadway to look out.

That group of townsmen across in front of the leather works seemed to have thinned out. Two of them had crossed the road and were walking in the direction of the jailhouse. The watcher said, 'Got the same idea. Bust into the jailhouse while the sheriff's at the eatery.'

Al Hopper winked at Asa. 'We're goin' to beat the hangman, partner.'

They led the animals out back, mounted in the alley and were turning away north-westerly when a man with a voice like a bear shouted an alarm. He was one of the pair who had gone to the jailhouse to drag out the prisoner for a lynching. He stepped to the open doorway of the jailhouse and roared to his friends in front of the harness works.

'They're gone, the whole lot of 'em!'

Within minutes townsmen were reacting, those who owned mounts went to get them, those who had no reason to own horses headed for the livery barn.

Barnum was in noisy, profane turmoil. Questions were shouted to which there were few answers. It wouldn't be long before the method and route of escape were known.

The Battleboro men went out and around leaving spirals of dust devils in their wake.

There was cause for delay in Barnum. Bonner Watkins had been left behind and agitated townsmen dragged him into the roadway. The lynching mood was aggravated until Maryanne yanked the arm of Barnum's foremost citizen, owner of the emporium, Andy Bartlett and despite his effort to shake her loose, forced him to stop long enough for her to say, 'He's not one of them. He was the partner of the redheaded man. They caught him out where those religious folks live. He was in their loft. They got him down. I expect they wanted to take him back to Battleboro with them, but that's just a guess. Andy, whatever else he is, he's not one of the men you want.'

The storekeeper, red and perspiring, got the attention of a burly man wearing sleeve cuffs and said, 'Willie, lock this one back in the jailhouse. He was a prisoner of the others. Hurry! Lock him up, get your horse and follow after us. *Hurry, damn it!*'

The hefty storekeeper turned to Maryanne. 'They'll be heading for Battleboro?'

Her answer was evasive. 'You can see their dust. They're riding in the opposite direction.'

There were mounted, armed men milling in the roadway, agitated and leaderless. The storekeeper went after his combination horse. By the time he returned to the centre of town a mob of horsemen were already raising dust in a pell mell rush. They didn't have to see the fleeing rangemen, they had standing dust banners to guide them.

In any horse race the pursued had more reason to ride hard than pursuers, but the distance separating both groups was little more than about a mile. Maybe a mile and a half.

Bob Whitney looked over his shoulder, they all did, but his immediate concern was direction. If they held to their present course they would eventually be within cannon range of the cultists.

If they made no attempt to make that diversion and continued as they were going all they could see ahead was unpopulated open country. There were occasional bosques of trees, and several boulder fields.

Behind them there arose a high-pitched yell, more of a wail than a shout. Someone wearing spurs with small rowels had one of the liveryman's animals which was as docile and obedient as a dog, unless his rider was wearing hooks. He had a powerful aversion to being spurred, which was neither common nor uncommon among horses, but this horse was a short-backed, leggy animal with little piggy eyes who could buck with the best of them. He sent his townsman rider through the air like a bird. It was this man's high-pitched wail that had carried to the fleeing rangemen.

No one had tried to count the pursuers. Numbers might ultimately be important but not until later.

10

A Near Thing

The pursuit neither gained nor lost ground for the first few miles and while a few shots were exchanged the range was great and the hurricane deck of a running horse mitigated the chance of anyone being hurt.

Range animals were not only physically capable, as a rule they were also tough with 'bottom' enough to widen the gap between livery animals, older, less willing.

But it took time. When the townsmen realized they were going to be out-distanced their initial reaction was to spur and quirt their mounts. Under this kind of treatment the horses gave their last spurt which was not enough. One of the townsmen slackened off, yelled for his companions to let up or they would chest founder the horses.

They slackened and watched the rangemen widen the gap until they were small in the distance.

With pursuit slackening Al Hopper let go with a triumphant yell. No one else did. They were free for the time being. They were also in territory none of them was familiar with. They drew down to a walk which gave their animals a breather.

There were mountains but they were distant, otherwise the land was grazing country. One rider making the crossing would be as noticeable as nearly a dozen would be.

When they came to a sump spring in the centre of several acres of overgrown marsh, they stopped to loosen cinches, remove bridles and tank up the horses, not to full capacity, just enough intake to replace sweat but not enough to colic their animals.

The men also drank, belly-down, using cupped hands. The 'breed slowly sat up with water dripping, squinted in several directions, sank to the ground again and remained there for some time before springing to his feet.

'Train!' he exclaimed. 'Coming up country!'

They had paralleled train tracks for several miles before drifting away from them. The tracks were a good mile south.

Al Hopper went to stand beside his horse, head raised like a sniffing coon dog.

Asa Tucker tipped down his hat, saw the distant spiral of rising smoke and called this to the attention of the others.

Walter Corrigan startled the others when he began bridling his horse as he said, 'We can stop it!'

At the blank looks he got, the taciturn man said, 'Block the track.'

Rory Kildare went to bridle and snug up. As he was doing this he disdainfully said, 'What in hell are you talkin' about, Walter?'

Corrigan was slow to answer. Junior

Roy did it for him. 'Stop the train, load us'n the horses aboard and get hauled so far they'll never find us.'

Al Hopper considered Junior Roy. 'Can't you hear it? It's comin' from the west in a beeline east toward Barnum.'

Walter Corrigan had gained enough time to speak again. 'If it's cattle cars it won't much matter.'

'It'll matter,' exclaimed Kildare. 'It'll take us to Barnum.'

This time Corrigan had an answer. 'It'll take us anywhere we want to go, with a gun muzzle in the train-driver's damned ear.'

Bruce Evans gave the order. 'Get astride. Al, lead off.'

Hopper took the lead, ignored the audible racket, concentrated on the smoke and set his gait for an interception a few miles south-east.

There were dissenters. There always were. On the ascent to Heaven there would be someone to squawk about how high they were getting.

Bruce Evans, Asa Tucker and the younger man Junior Roy rode stirrup with Evans in the middle. They rode in silence alternately watching the 'breed and the visible spiral of dirty dark smoke.

When they could distantly make out the train with its trailing slatted cattle cars they followed Hopper's example and boosted their animals into a lope.

The country was open, flat and occasionally showed little bands of cattle.

No one called ahead to ask how they would stop the train. Al Hopper's palpable confidence was inspiring and simultaneously doubtful. The 'breed was an ingenious individual. He had proved that several times, the last time when he'd hit Bonner Watkins with his stone-handled boot knife, but the huge iron horse belching smoke couldn't be stopped that easily. In fact it couldn't be stopped even with blowing steam and locking the binders in less than a mile.

They gauged the distance when they reached the tracks. The train wouldn't reach their position for about fifteen minutes.

They clustered until the 'breed yanked out a dirty bandanna, cut his arm, let the bandanna absorb blood, then threw his hat aside, tied the bloody bandanna around his head and yelled for the others to dismount, some of them to lie on the ground and without waiting to see if he would be obeyed boosted his animal into a lope toward the right side of the oncoming engine.

Asa understood and swung to the ground, yelled for the others to follow his example and when they were dismounted he pointed fingers, told the men he'd indicated to sprawl in the grass and set the example by going down only a few yards from the tracks.

The 'breed waved wildly as he came beside the engineer's side of the train and yelled. It was doubtful if the engineer understood the words: 'In'ians, massacree!' but the bloody sleeve and headband were sufficient. The engineer exhausted steam, eased on the binders and yelled to his stoker to get their weapons.

A brakeman, old, bent and grizzled, craned in Hopper's direction to yell. The 'breed ignored him and continued his harangue of the engineer.

The brakeman climbed to the top of the fuel car and put a cupped hand to his eyes. After a moment he climbed down, grabbed the engineer's arm and said, 'There's some hurt fellers.'

The engineer was on the wrong side of the cab to see the Battleboro men. He yelled at the brakeman. 'What's that danged In'ian yellin' about?'

'There was some kind of fight. Look out over here; there's some hurt fellers in the grass. I'll set the wheel brakes.'

Even with a string of empty slatted cattle cars it was not easy to stop the train. The engineer blew his ballast of white hot steam about the same time the iron wheels on the steel rails made an almost deafening sound as they ground to a halt.

The wizened brakeman climbed down heading for the scattered strangers. Al Hopper met him in front of the engine smiling like a tame ape. That irritated the older man. 'You goddamn tomahawks got a miserable sense of humour. There's hurt fellers . . . '

Hopper didn't cock the six-gun but he aimed it at the brakeman's head.

The old man stopped stone still. The prone men got to their feet, three of them went around to the far side of the engine where the engineer was standing like a stone squinting out the left side of his engine and holding a Winchester rifle.

Junior Roy climbed up, tapped the engineer and when he turned Junior Roy cocked the six-gun he was holding ten inches from the engineer's face.

The fireman was too stunned to move as two more armed men climbed to the cab. Only the brakeman wasn't speechless for an excellent reason, he had been on trains stopped by outlaws three times. Two of those times Al Jennings and his brother were the highwaymen.

He swore at the Battleboro men, even shook a wizened fist. Otherwise he accepted what was happening; this was the fourth time!

Al Hopper, still wearing the askew bloody bandanna yelled for the first cattle car to be opened and the ramp jimmied into place which required most of the time after the train was stopped.

The fireman and engineer did not leave the cab. The brakeman, already on the ground, swore and gestured without once asking questions.

He didn't need answers. He was certain a band of outlaws would only have stopped the train and were loading their horses to get out of the country.

Loading the horses was troublesome, some horses balked at the idea of stepping on anything that reverberated under weight, or sounded hollow.

This delay shortened tempers. Some-where out of sight there would be mounted manhunters. By the time the door could be closed and latched with the animals inside, Bruce Evans was sweating and nervous.

Three men were in the slatted car with the horses. Three more took watchful positions in the tender. Bruce, Asa and the 'breed were in the cab where the engineer watched gauges until a fair head of steam was up, then eased the train ahead.

It was difficult to be heard so there was very little talk, except for the irate brakeman, he cursed everyone and everything.

Disarming the train crew was accomplished, the engineer was told not to stop at Barnum, to keep going easterly.

He looked at Asa. Being accustomed to speak loudly he said, 'That's where I got to stop. There'll be a corral full of cattle waiting.'

The answer was rough and brusque.

'Just keep goin' right on past town or get thrown off.'

It worked, the engineer and his companion kept the fire box filled and made respectable speed.

The engineer, a grey, grizzled professional, overcame his anxiety and, as was his custom, leaned out of the right side.

He had been tooling trains almost eighteen years; when he had a decent head of steam up he ignored everything but his job.

The horses were uncomfortable. None of them had been confined in a cattle car before and while they could not get out past the timber siding and could do nothing else, the three men with them had to avoid getting their feet stepped on.

The wizened brakeman came up beside Bruce Evans and said, 'They'll get you. Ain't an outlaw been born that don't get caught.'

Bruce fished in a pocket, offered the makings and the brakeman demonstrated how long he'd ridden in windy cabs by putting his back to the windy places to roll and light a smoke.

As he returned the makings, he asked a question in a slightly modified tone of voice, 'You boys rob a bank?' When Bruce shook his head the older man nodded. 'A bullion stage, eh?'

Bruce raised his voice. 'We didn't rob anythin'. We just got a good reason for gettin' as far from Barnum as we can.'

The old timer inhaled, exhaled, eyed Bruce pensively, shrugged and went to lean out the far side opening. After a moment he yelled to the engineer, 'You see it, Clement?'

The engineer yelled back. 'I see it, an' they're goin' to be real upset when we go right on through.'

He was right. It was customary for trains to slacken speed a mile westerly. This train not only didn't release any steam, it kept right on going. Some horsemen sat their saddles like carvings. The train was not going to stop. Their corralled beef was not going to be loaded.

One man drew his six-gun and fired it into the air. Inside the cab the sound of a gunshot could not compete with the train's regular noise.

Another rider reined toward the engine yelling and flagging with his hat. The only acknowledgement the rider got was from the brakeman; he threw out the stub of his smoke and expectorated.

Barnum's citizens came to the centre of the road. Some boys whooped, hollered and waved, the adults watched the train pass the loading pens with gaping mouths and round eyes.

Barnum had been a shipping centre for a dozen years. Trains stopped for a refill at the water tower if for no other reason. Not this train. With the engineer on his seat, arms raised to touch the whistle and the brakeman standing between the cab and the tender holding to steel on both sides, only the fireman might have had time to yell at the watchers and he was busy keeping the fire box full.

The pens and loading chute were a little shy of being a half-mile from town. Range cattle who had never seen nor heard a railroad train before invariably panicked. They couldn't break out, not against fir logs as large around as a man, but that didn't prevent them from trying, charging, bellowing, acting wild-eyed enough to trample anyone foolish to get inside which no one did nor ever had. The cattle made enough racket and commotion to cause a diversion, at least among the mounted men who had brought them to Barnum to be shipped east.

What was later recalled as a prolonged interlude of noise, confusion and bewilderment did not in fact require more than fifteen minutes from the time the train should have slackened to stop until it went straight past Barnum billowing smoke and making the ground reverberate.

Andy Bartlett, Barnum's storekeeper, sore and upset over losing sight of the outlaws as part of the town posse, was standing near the lower end of town not far from the smithy as the train ran past. He watched empty cattle cars whip by, counted five and went to a nearby stump and sat down, was still sitting there when townsmen came to the lower end of town where they could see the train better. Only when Sheriff Holt appeared did the storekeeper arise from his stump. 'Will, did you see 'em?'

Holt frowned. 'See who?'

'That second car had horses in it an' that loudmouthed rangeman you had locked up. The feller named Taunton.'

Sheriff Holt considered the storekeeper for a moment before shifting his gaze to the distant last car on the train.

'Are you sure, Andy?'

'As sure as I'm standing here. He was between two horses leanin' to look out.'

Sheriff Holt left the area heading

203

for the telegrapher's cubby-hole of an office.

The telegrapher was cocked back reading a dogeared newspaper which he put aside when Holt walked in and said, 'Wireless east to Burley to stop that train . . . you deaf, Ralph? *Stop that train!*'

The telegrapher went to work with his instrument. When he was finished he looked up. 'All right, they got it. Sheriff . . . ?'

'Because them jail-breakin', outlaw, sons of bitches was on it, with their horses.'

The telegrapher waited until the lawman was gone then reread what he had telegraphed and went to stand by the window facing the roadway.

What he did not know was that the town he had telegraphed to named Burley was thirty-five miles east of the town which had no telegraph named Battleboro, the destination of the men who had commandeered a train.

It required very little time for what

the storekeeper had told the sheriff to spread. The storekeeper, as with many of his kind, was the local source of information on just about every subject.

This time what he had to relate caused an understandable degree of excitement. Among the posse riders who had lost a horse race with the Battleboro men this latest scrap of information stimulated enough inflamed wrath to cause Sheriff Holt to lock up early and head for home. But even there he was not safe. Irate citizens hammered at his door, something the lawman ignored as best he could. His daughter, in her best lawyerly attitude, made no attempt to placate anyone; she instead urged the formation of a posse to follow the train, an idea that was not unanimously accepted. There had never in all history been a saddle animal that could keep up with nor catch up to a steam engine pulling the railroad company's variety of wagons.

For the men on the commandeered

train, the smaller Barnum got to their rear the more relieved they felt. It was impossible to talk much but Asa, Bruce Evans and Al Hopper made the effort. For Bruce Evans, the immediate future, reaching home country, was more important than anything else, at least for the time being. Asa Tucker had to repeat himself three times before Evans answered. 'All I can tell you, Asa, is that your brother was conscious an' bein' cared for when I last saw him.'

Asa said, 'I'm goin' back. That son of a bitch Watkins deserves a killing.'

Evans rolled his eyes. The only reason he and his companions had raided Barnum was to free Asa Tucker. So far no one had been bad hurt but his waltz wasn't over yet. 'Hold off until we see how your brother is holdin' up.'

Asa nodded without conviction. 'Until we get home, but that murderin' son of a —'

'Asa, that's a hard-nosed lawman back yonder. Let's just hang an' rattle until we know what he's done.'

After a pause Evans also said, 'I got a bad feelin', Asa.'

'What about? I didn't murder that drunk bastard.'

'Not that,' Evans countered. 'We took you out of a jailhouse where you'd been committed for trial. I don't know much law but seems to me we put ourselves right damn in the middle, between a local lawman we defied, an' US marshals.'

'US marshals? We didn't do anything against federal law.'

'Yes we did, Asa. We commandeered a steam train an' I know for a fact train robbery is against federal law. Wait a minute. You're goin' to say what we did was justified. Maybe it was. You'n I think it was, but federal lawmen might think otherwise an' I can tell you, goin' head to head with federal marshals is like gettin' kicked in the head by a mule. We'd lose.'

Asa's brow wrinkled. 'It wasn't breakin' federal law. They was goin' to kill me. It was all set up. If they succeeded I'd have got murdered, not that redheaded bastard.'

Bruce forced a smile. 'You'n me know that. So do the fellers as rode with us, but that's not how the federal law will look at it. To them we commandeered a train . . . I think we're gettin' close to home.'

Evans wasn't sure of this but between the two of them their disagreement was too wide to be resolved.

Alamo Taunton yelled from the horse car. The distance and the noise made it impossible to understand but his gesture was clear enough.

Battleboro was in sight far northerly, just barely, and this day was slowly drawing to a close. The sun was still up there but it was no longer red, it was fading into a shade of pale rust, the indication that dusk was close.

They stopped the train using cocked pistols. As always the train blew steam and its restrained steel wheels rolling at reduced speed over steel rails made the kind of sound that put teeth on edge.

Off loading was accomplished with less difficulty than loading had been.

For the first time, the engineer climbed out and stood with his stoker and brakeman watching in silence from expressions set in stone.

The wizened brakeman approached the 'breed and said, 'You ain't heard the last of this by a long shot.'

Hopper smiled from his saddle. 'I sure hope not, old man. I got sort of fond of train-ridin'. I was never on a train before.'

'You'll get another train ride,' the old man said venomously. 'It's about a three-day ride to the Yuma Penitentiary.'

Hopper's smile lingered. 'In'ians win, old man. Put us in prison where they'll feed us an' we'll sleep in dry beds while folks like you'll pay for it.'

The saddle animals were still 'high' but getting them unloaded had helped to quiet them a little.

As the Battleboro men swung astride, unsociable, taciturn Walter Corrigan rode up to the engineer and extended his hand. 'I never rode a steam car before. You steered this one real well an' I'm obliged.'

The engineer extended his hand slowly, shook and freed his hand. All without a word.

It required considerable time to build up enough steam to run the train in reverse all the way back to Barnum. Walter Corrigan watched sitting twisted in the saddle with his left hand on the rump of his horse and shook his head. It required real skill to back a saddle horse for any distance in a straight line. That belching, ugly noisy machine never wavered nor left its tracks.

Rory Kildare loped ahead, left his animal at the livery barn and hastened to his saloon where the stocky, pock-faced individual he usually hired to run things while he was away, looked surprised when Kildare came through the spindle doors. He was dirty, unshaven, rumpled and tired looking.

As the stand-by man began untying

his apron, Kildare shook his head. 'Stay with it, Emory. I'm goin' home, maybe take an all-over bath an' sleep until next week.'

A gangling, weathered and lined rangeman with a shot glass halfway to his mouth said, 'I don't know about the rest of it, Rory, but even from over here I can tell you sure need the bath.'

11

The Show Down

Birch Tucker's bandaged head had been sheared to the bone on one side. He had a room at the hotel where the caféman brought food; otherwise, with his headache gone and less bloodshot in both eyes he looked and acted sufficiently recovered. His brother's first words were, 'You need a shave,' and the darker man made a sardonic smile as he said, 'Where's my horse?'

'Down at the livery barn. He wasn't hurt. Birch, the redheaded renegade that shot you is dead but his weasel-faced partner is over in the Barnum jailhouse. We left him there; we had to move fast when we made a run for it.'

Birch motioned toward the only chair

and said, 'Tell me about it.'

Birch Tucker wasn't the only one. At Kildare's pleasure palace several of the other men were willing to talk in exchange for cough medicine.

None of them got to bed before the wee hours nor were they abroad the following day until noon.

Claude Garret, the general store proprietor in Battleboro and the town marshal, listened to Alamo Taunton whose recitation had about as much to do with Barnum's sheriff and his fee-lawyer daughter arguing as it had to do with other aspects of the trouble over yonder.

Alamo had spent most of his time in the Barnum country locked in the jailhouse with Asa Tucker.

When he finished, the town marshal looked steadily at Alamo and said, 'I know Will Holt. He's not a forgivin' man. You want some advice, get on your horse and don't even look back for two months.'

It was sound advice, but when a

nose count was made, one survivor of the Barnum ruckus was missing. Junior Roy had drawn his wages and left town the morning after the full crew had returned. What folks thought went unsaid when Sheriff Holt's beefy deputy Bud Lange rode into Battleboro the morning of the third day.

He was recognized by survivors and consequently word spread fast.

His visit to the jailhouse was noticed, with smiles, as Battleboro's town marshal had departed for Albuquerque the day before to visit his daughter down there whose husband was a combination town carpenter and coffin-maker. The marshal had told several acquaintances he'd been promising his daughter he'd visit her for three years.

No one made an effort to recollect ever having heard the marshal mention a daughter, nor for the time being did it matter. Battleboro would be without a lawman at a time folks were confident some kind of retaliatory action would be forthcoming from the

Barnum country as they watched the beefy man ride back the way he had come.

At a gathering of Battleboro's town council it was unanimously decided to appoint Birch Tucker temporary lawman. Even Rory Kildare had been in favour and it was common knowledge that Rory did not like Indians, full blood or the diluted kind.

Sam Brown, the head Indian of the local stagecompany's corralyard, also antipathetic toward tomahawks, particularly toward Asa Tucker, had joined the unanimous vote as the last councilman to do so. His most recent reason for getting his hackles up was that he had seen Asa Tucker talking to his daughter in front of the Garret emporium.

When Birch Tucker was sworn in and had the badge pinned on his shirt, despite his complaints that he wasn't qualified, knew nothing about enforcing the law and didn't feel altogether recovered from his bullet crease, he might as well have been talking to a rock.

Birch, his brother the fugitive, and at least two dozen other people were convinced that as soon as he could Sheriff Holt would appear in Battleboro, and they were right.

When the whip for Sam Brown's east-west stage run reached town he brought some electrifying information. Sheriff Holt was half a day's ride from Battleboro and his deputy Bud Lange was with him. It did not require much sense to figure that after Bud's appearance in Battleboro and his discovery that the town marshal was gone, Sheriff Holt would feel reinforced in his mission, whatever that was, and again, folks in Battleboro had no doubt about that.

What really greased the fry pan was when the coachman said Will Holt's entourage looked like a small army. The whip had counted eight riders not including Holt nor his deputy.

Birch's dark eyes widened. 'Ten?'

Fidgety Sam Brown suggested that Battleboro organize; prepare to fight man for man.

One councilman, a recent addition to Battleboro, a combination midwife, horse doctor and apothecary, thought they ought to ride out and palaver, not wait for Holt and his companions to reach town.

There was an argument about that and the apothecary did not press his suggestion. He was from back East somewhere.

But one issue was resolved; word was passed that Sheriff Holt and his companions should not be allowed to take Asa Tucker or anyone else back to Barnum, no matter what legal authority they might have, or pretend to have.

A rider from a cow outfit miles east of town reached Rory Kildare's saloon dry as a bone with more electrifying news. He had ridden a mile or such a matter with the Barnum men and had seen two of those little round badges on the shirts of two of Holt's companions.

The kind of badges US marshals and their deputies wore.

Bruce Evans was sent for at his ranch. He reached town an hour or so before dusk and was immediately informed of what portended.

During his absence his ranch had suffered. He was still irritable when he reached Battleboro. It did not help his disposition that what looked like a war was shaping up.

Birch and Asa talked at the jailhouse office. Asa was willing to surrender to Holt. His brother only halfheartedly opposed the idea. The final agreement was that they would do nothing until Sheriff Holt reached town.

With evening settling, Asa made another of his earlier mistakes. Because he expected to be arrested and returned to Barnum he caught Betsy Brown on her way home from the corralyard office and not only explained what he intended to do, and why, which was to avoid a turkey shoot in town, he also told her how he felt and that he wanted to marry her.

At that moment it seemed not to matter to either of them that Betsy's father had also closed up for the night and, as was his custom, had started across to Kildare's saloon for a night cap, and stopped stone-still in the middle of the road looking up the plankwalk where his daughter and Asa Tucker were talking. Even the diminishing light of a dying day did not obscure the fact that Asa and Betsy kissed.

Sam Brown let out a roar that would have put a wild bull to shame and started on an angling hike in the direction of the two young people.

They weren't the only ones who heard the bellow of rage, several of Rory Kildare's patrons and Rory himself came out past the spindle doors looking left and right. They saw Betsy's father striding purposefully with both fists clenched.

There were other spectators who saw Betsy step in front of Asa Tucker to face her red-faced, knotted-fisted father.

The ample wife of a freighter gave her bearded husband a hard shove. 'Stop him,' she exclaimed. Her husband looked around. If he'd had wings he couldn't have gotten there before Sam Brown caught Asa Tucker.

Birch had heard the bellow, went to stand in the jailhouse door, forehead creased with worry. What he saw was not what had worried him. It was not men from Barnum, it was Sam Brown reaching to roughly shove his daughter aside.

Birch walked quickly to intervene but, as with the freighter, he would be unable to get that far up the road in time.

Nor was he. In a voice harshened by anger the corralyard boss told his daughter to get out of the way and when she stood her ground, white-faced but obdurate, her father flung out one hand, grabbed and twisted. The girl lost her balance and fell. From in front of the saloon it looked as though her father had struck her.

Several of Rory's customers growled and left the plankwalk on their way across the road. The distance wasn't great but it might as well have been. The corralyard boss only shifted direction before firing his right fist.

Asa leaned far enough to avoid the strike. He tried to say something. The corralyard boss rushed him. This time, with not enough manoeuvring ground, Asa half turned sideways and lashed out.

The blow lacked the power it should have had but it caught Sam Brown in the chest, high up, and stopped his rush.

For three seconds Asa had the respite he needed, and wasted it. Instead of following up his first strike he tried to talk, and the corralyard boss heaved a little to the left side of the plankwalk and came back with his right fist cocked.

Later it was said among spectators

that Asa made no move to avoid the blow; it was almost as though he wanted to be hit.

Whatever the reason the blow connected. Asa staggered backwards off the plankwalk and Betsy, rumpled and dirty from her fall, got between her father and Asa Tucker. He reached as he'd done before to get her out of the way but this time she moved faster. The sound of her open palm striking her father's face was audible to the watchers in front of Kildare's saloon and at least one man harshly laughed.

A burly bearded freighter from in front of the saloon caught Betsy's father from behind, whirled him and struck. The corralyard boss doubled over, both hands protecting his middle.

The freighter stood wide-legged with both hands at his sides. He said, 'You woman-hittin' son of a bitch, come on. I'm goin' to break half the bones in your carcass. *Come on!*'

Birch Tucker knew the freighter from

years back. He said, 'Green, I'll take it from here.'

The freighter was slow relaxing and responding. He said, 'I never liked that sniffin' ratty bastard. Did you see him hit his girl?'

Birch hadn't seen Betsy get slapped but something had happened, there was grass in her hair, her face was flushed and she was facing her father like a bitch cougar.

Birch got in front of the freighter. Green Hamison had a reputation as a hand fighter. Birch wagged his head. 'You did right, Green, now it's up to me.'

The freighter glared at the corralyard boss and started past toward the roadway. He stopped once, turned and said, 'I ever even hear of you hittin' a woman again an' I'll scalp you alive!'

Betsy ignored her father, took Asa by the arm and started walking. Among the onlookers an old man called after them, 'Boy, watch your back.'

Sam Brown straightened up. The punch to his soft parts had hurt. When Birch started to speak, the corralyard boss brushed past, went down to his office, walked in and slammed the door after himself.

Across the road, the spectators trooped back inside following Rory Kildare. Birch shook his head and started back toward the jailhouse. He almost made it before a teenage lad atop the general store where his pa had told him to go, put two fingers in his mouth and made a whistle which was audible all over town. The lad's father caught up with Birch and said, 'They're just outside town,' and walked briskly away.

Birch didn't enter the jailhouse. He stepped over to the tie rack out front, yanked loose the tie-down over his holstered Colt and leaned, gazing southward.

He seemed to be the only person in sight the full length of the roadway, but that was an illusion. There were watchers the full length of town on both sides of the road including women and a scattering of children. The men watchers were armed with an assortment of weapons ranging from shotguns loaded with pellets for bringing geese down — to the Yankee import who doctored horses and delivered babies. He stood in the doorway of his shop with a nickel-plated, five-shot handgun visible in the front of his britches.

Sheriff Holt rode stirrup with a bull-necked, burly, mustachioed individual astride one of those 800-pound, short-backed, quarter running horses out of Texas. This man had his deputy US marshal's badge in plain sight. Behind him rode another man wearing the same kind of badge, otherwise, excepting beefy Bud Lange, the well-armed riders looked like dragooned rangemen of Barnum townsmen.

They rode bunched up, expressionless and silent. They had reason to act that way, their entrance into Battleboro was like riding into a ghost town. But for an occasional stray dog the roadway was empty except for the solemn-faced 'breed with the town marshal's badge leaning impassively on a tie rack in front of the jailhouse.

The aggressive-looking deputy marshal riding beside Will Holt leaned to say something which the sheriff answered cryptically and jutted his jaw in Birch Tucker's direction.

This happened as they were passing the livery barn whose proprietor distinctly heard the sheriff say, 'That's his brother.'

They ignored the livery barn which was unusual. It was customary for strangers to put up their animals before doing anything else.

As they approached Birch Tucker, he straightened up and waited. Sheriff Holt halted, resting both hands atop the apple and nodded. It was an interesting meeting. Neither Birch Tucker nor Will Holt were talkative individuals.

A dog fight up near Kildare's place created a brief diversion. A lanky boy came out of nowhere, grabbed one of the dogs by the scruff and led it away.

Sheriff Holt cleared his throat and leaned to dismount. Birch Tucker said, 'Stay up there, Mr Holt.'

The moustachioed, burly federal lawman said, 'Where's Asa Tucker?'

Birch, still wearing a cloth bandage, considered the lawman. 'You got a name, mister?'

It wasn't the kind of answer the square-jawed older man expected. 'Name's Barney Colton. What's yours?'

Birch offered a delayed reply. 'Tucker. Birch Tucker. You got a reason for bringin' this bunch of armed gents to Battleboro, Mr Colton?'

The burly man's small eyes, the colour of gunmetal, were fixed on Birch Tucker. 'You heard the sheriff: where's Asa Tucker?'

Birch kept his dark gaze on the federal lawman. 'Why do you want to know?'

This was about as much hard talk

as the burly man would take. He, too, leaned to dismount and this time Battleboro's newly appointed town marshal said the same thing he'd said to the sheriff. 'Stay up there, Mr Colton.'

The burly man came down hard on the left side of his horse and waited. Birch didn't prolong the wait. 'Get back up there, Mr Colton.'

'An' if I don't!'

'I'll lock you up.'

'What charge, Marshal?'

'How about drunk'n disorderly?'

Colton snorted. 'It's got to be better'n that, 'breed.'

Across the road, in the vicinity of the general store, someone loudly cocked both barrels of a scattergun. For several seconds no one spoke or moved. Marshal Colton sneered. 'Mister, I represent the fed'ral law an' I don't like back-shootin' bushwhackers. For the last time, where's Asa Tucker!'

Unexpectedly, Sam Brown came down from his corralyard carrying a shotgun with a fourteen-inch barrel. He provided another diversion. He didn't say a word, not even when he stopped in front of the jailhouse, raised his sawn-off shotgun and pointed it at the US deputy marshal. Then he said. 'Ten seconds to get back on that horse.'

The burly, bull-necked man glared. 'Or what, sodbuster?'

Before the corralyard boss could answer, Birch Tucker said, 'Leave it be, Sam. Point that thing in some other direction.'

Brown acted as though he had not heard. He didn't lower the gun and he answered the bull-built lawman. When he spoke, those who knew Sam Brown heard the higher pitch and worried. Sam Brown was known for his unpredictable temperament. 'I'll blow your gawddamn head off!'

Sheriff Holt stiffened in his saddle. He was a good judge of men. His private and unspoken assessment of the corralyard boss was accurate. 'Get back astride,' he told the deputy US marshal, who turned slowly and scowled at Sheriff Holt. 'No damned clodhopper was ever born braced me down,' he growled.

Men were watching from different places and could not hear what was being said, didn't have to. Body language was as good if not better than spoken language. Someone loudly whistled. This time it wasn't the lad who'd been on the roof of the store, it was his father who had taught his boy how to whistle.

The whistler emerged from a weathered house, jerked his head and also started walking from the upper end of Battleboro.

The head jerk was a signal. Other armed men appeared, some from stores, some from houses, a few from the back alleys on both sides of town.

The men on horseback watched this accumulation of armed men heading toward them and did not move, which was wise. The mood was easily interpreted. One false move and all hell was going to bust loose.

Deputy Marshal Colton turned, toed in and swung up into his saddle. His expression was the same, defiant to the core.

The ten Barnum riders were pretty well boxed in by what looked to be eighteen or twenty townsmen on foot.

Sheriff Holt and his deputy exchanged a look. Bud Lange addressed Birch Tucker.

'They got a warrant for Asa.'

'What charge, Bud?'

'Federal warrant for train robbery.'

Birch regarded the square-jawed man with the drooping dragoon moustache. 'No one robbed a train, Mr Colton.'

'They commandeered it, scairt hell out of its crew an' — '

'They didn't rob it. Somethin' else, Mr Colton: ask the sheriff about that charge against my brother for murder.'

'I already did; why else would I be here? Accordin' to the law Asa Tucker murdered that other feller.'

Bruce Evans who was in the surround, spoke loudly enough for everyone to hear him. 'They went out into the roadway to settle things. The fellow named Arnold . . . Marshal, they was facin' each other. Arnold wasn't fast enough. You want to know why? Ask the sheriff.'

'I know. He told me. It was still murder.'

'The feller named Bonner Watkins didn't kill Asa when he was supposed to. That's why the other feller got killed. It was a set-up ambush that went wrong.'

Colton placed a hand on the rump of his Texas horse and twisted to face Bruce Evans. 'Mister, I got a warrant. You'n me don't have to agree or disagree. I got a warrant an' the rest of it after I serve my warrant is up to the judge.'

Colton faced forward, small, cold eyes fixed on Birch Tucker.

Before either man could speak Asa

came down the plankwalk with the tie-down lashed over his holster. When he was close enough he introduced himself to the federal marshal.

'I'm Asa Tucker.'

12

Interruptions

No one was more surprised than Asa's brother. He stood looking at the younger man like he'd lost his tongue, but the federal deputy, accustomed to acting quickly, said, 'Shed that pistol, boy.' Dishevelled Betsy Brown came down the plankwalk with her gaze fixed on Asa. Because Asa too, stood motionless, the federal deputy repeated it. 'Shed that pistol. *Now!*'

Sam Brown took one step closer with his cocked shotgun. His daughter ignored them all, stood beside Asa and said, 'If you go I go with you.'

Her father reacted typically. He hoisted the shotgun a fraction as though to address the burly lawman. Those who knew Sam Brown heard the slightly higher pitch of his voice.

Birch Tucker moved between the glaring mounted lawman and Sam Brown, slowly raised a hand to force the shotgun down.

Sheriff Holt was white in the face. Behind him, his deputy cleared his throat before saying, 'Sheriff, I quit,' and dismounted to stand beside his horse.

One of the possemen spoke to the man beside him. 'Jack . . . ?'

The man spoken to eased up on his reins and answered without taking his eyes off the men up front, closest to the tie rack. 'Yeah. This ain't our war.'

That rider turned his animal and addressed a townsman. 'Where's the saloon?'

The townsman didn't answer, he raised an arm pointing northward. As the two rebellious possemen left their companions, a third posseman addressed Sheriff Holt. 'You said this'd be a turkey shoot. Don't look like it to me.'

The second federal deputy turned.

'Lily-livered sons of bitches; why don't you all quit!'

Only one other posseman followed the first two and he rode in their wake.

Marshal Colton and Sam Brown ignored everything but each other, for the federal lawman a wise thing to do since the corralyard boss was still holding his shotgun. Colton spoke to the sheriff. 'Is that him, Sheriff?'

Holt nodded in Asa's direction and the pair of federal officers dismounted.

That burly freighter named Green Hamison went to stand with Asa and Betsy Brown. Three other townsmen did the same. One of them had a Remington long-barrelled rifle in his hand. This man said, 'You boys better be a hell of a lot tougher'n you look. You lay a hand on young Tucker . . .' He didn't finish it. He didn't have to.

It was a Mexican standoff, one of those times when men would be damned if they did and damned if they didn't.

Bud Lange, the beefy Barnum deputy, whose brother had wanted him to go into the leather business for the best of all reasons; leather workers stayed warm in winter, cool in summer and didn't get into trouble, swung heavily to the ground looking unhappily resolute, handed off his reins and went to stand with the federal lawman and Sheriff Holt. His gaze moved from Asa to Birch whom he had known and liked for some years. Birch returned the look as he quietly said, 'Mr Colton, you're goin' to get yourself hurt if you try it.'

The burly man answered without taking his eyes off Asa; he was a manhunter with scars to prove it and no cow-town lily-livers were going to back him down. He ignored the warning and reached to grab Asa's arm.

Someone who smelled strongly of sage, sweat and whiskey spun the burly man around and hit him hard.

A posseman went for his handgun and Sam Brown aimed high and squeezed off both barrels of his shotgun. It started a running squealing, bucking exhibition with posse riders fighting to control terrified animals. One man went off in a spreadeagle fall. A terrified horse charged through the loose surround, scattering townsmen, struck the opposite plankwalk and broke past both doors of the general store, leaving the rider hanging briefly in the air where he'd been stopped by the topmost door jamb before he fell.

Birch brushed Bud Lange with his six-gun barrel. The beefy man turned, let his breath out and stepped over Marshal Colton to go sit on a bench out front of the jailhouse looking totally stunned.

Three possemen had runaways on their hands. When a terrified horse gets the bit between his tusks and grinders the strongest man on earth can't control him.

Two Barnum riders left their saddles, clung desperately to their reins, got dragged a piece before the horses stopped, wide-legged and quivering.

An expressionless Sheriff Will Holt got the hefty US marshal to his feet, got him to the bench and propped him beside Bud, who looked at the sheriff with dull eyes and said, 'I quit, Mr Holt,' removed his badge and dropped it.

Sheriff Holt ignored the badge. Of all the agitated individuals out front of the jailhouse he was the calmest. He said, 'You keep the badge. I'm quittin'. I thought on it on the ride over here, I don't need what goes with the job.'

Sam Brown reloaded his scattergun. His daughter approached with tears and her father did what every man-jack in Battleboro would have bet his best boots the corralyard boss wouldn't do.

He dropped the shotgun and held out his arms. Betsy went to him crying her heart out. He stroked her hair as he said, 'You marry him, Bets. He knows horses an' I need a good man at the yard.'

'Papa, I love him.'

Sam Brown looked over his only child's head at Asa, raised his voice just slightly and said, 'Be good to her, boy.'

Birch tapped Sheriff Holt on the shoulder. The sheriff had one hand against the federal lawman's chest to keep him from toppling off the bench but he turned his head.

Birch said, 'Where's the other one?'

'What other one?'

'The partner to the son of a bitch that shot me.'

Sheriff Holt removed his supporting hand, the federal officer curled forward in slow motion and fell off the bench. He was ignored.

'I turned him loose, Birch.' At the look on the darker man's face he also said, 'I had no charge to hold him on. He didn't use his gun an' as far as I know there's no dodger out on him. Birch, I do my sheriffin' accordin' to the law books. The best I could've done was hold him for disturbin' the peace.'

'Where did he go?'

Sheriff Holt was tired and looked it. 'Leave it be. He'll get his some day. I don't know where he went. Birch, it was the other one that shot you.'

The dark man turned away. Several townsmen were laughing as they watched a posse rider fight his crazed mount to a standstill.

The horse bogged his head and bucked until the posseman got his head up and squaw-reined him as hard as he could until the single rein he was using had the animal's neck so far to one side its head was almost in his lap. The horse gave a mighty lunge and fell, its rider kicked loose both feet and also fell but wasn't pinned. He drew his six-gun to shoot the horse when Asa ran at him. He knocked the posse rider aside. He almost fell, he'd been straddling the horse.

His pistol went sailing. Asa cocked his right fist and the shaken posseman threw up an arm.

No one was laughing now, now

they were holding their breath. Asa leathered his weapon, extended a hand and got the rider to his feet, turned and walked back where his brother and the Barnum lawman had been watching.

Asa handed his six-gun to Will Holt, looked briefly at Betsy and said, 'I'll be back, Bets. Some day . . . Sheriff . . . ?'

Holt looked from the gun in his hand to young Tucker, handed back the weapon and went over where some of his companions were standing, some were bruised, they had torn shirts and had lost their hats. Holt said, 'Let's get the horses, lads.'

From back by the bench, the federal lawman spoke in an unsteady tone of voice. 'You got him, Sheriff?'

Holt turned. 'You want him, Mr Colton, you take him. Me, I quit. I'm goin' home.'

Colton arose from the bench. His legs lacked a little of doing what legs were supposed to do. He looked around. 'Where's the son of a bitch that hit me from behind?'

Green Hamison spat amber, pushed past to the plankwalk and stopped. 'I hit you. You better rest up a spell.'

They faced each other over a distance of something like fifteen feet, Hamison waiting, Marshal Colton bleakly expressionless. Eventually he turned, saw the corralyard boss and said, 'Is that your shotgun, mister?'

Brown answered curtly. 'It is. If you want to know did I stampede the horses with it, yes, sir, I did. Both barrels.'

Green Hamison glanced at Birch, gave his head a slight, contemptuous wag and walked away. It didn't fool folks but it helped a man avoid getting hurt by changing the subject.

Rory Kildare was in the middle of the road when he raised his voice. 'First round on me, gents,' and started slow-pacing in the direction of his saloon. He had takers, townsmen and possemen, not all but enough.

Marshal Colton saw his partner looking at him and said, 'I'll look him up. Right now I'll set here for a spell . . . whoever he is he can hit like gettin' kicked by an army mule.'

The younger deputy US marshal watched men streaming up the centre of the road in the direction of the saloon and followed them, his back to those still in front of the jailhouse so they couldn't see his look of disgust.

Sam Brown retrieved his scattergun and straightened up grinning. When he spoke he addressed Asa. 'I gave them boys a handful of trouble, didn't I?'

Asa grinned. 'I'd say you kept a killin' from happenin'.' Asa cleared his throat, threw a darting look at Betsy and asked her father a question. 'Was you joshin' or did you mean it about needin' a hand at the corralyard?'

Sam Brown also flitted a glance at his daughter before replying. 'Better talk it out with your brother. You can't help on the ranch an' work in the corralyard both.'

Asa faced Betsy and smiled. She returned the smile but it was difficult. She had just gone through an experience she would never forget.

Sheriff Holt, the pair of federal lawmen, Birch Tucker, Bruce Evans, Asa Tucker and the Barnum deputy entered the jailhouse office.

When the burly officer seemed about to speak, Sheriff Holt spoke first. 'My daughter said Bonner Watkins couldn't be held. The only thing that tied him to the redheaded feller was Bonner's word an' she could make a case that the redheaded feller, drunk or sober, just wasn't fast enough. Mister Tucker, far as I'm concerned neither of them fellers was any loss.'

Marshal Colton spoke up gruffly. 'That shooting over yonder's the local law's business. What I got a warrant for is train robbery. That's the government's business. You want to know why?'

Birch nodded without speaking.

'Because trains cross state lines. Train robbery that happens in a place like Battleboro is the local law's problem. When the train crosses into another state, mister, then it becomes the fed'ral government's job an' that's why me'n my friend are here. And someday I'm goin' to look up that feller who hit me from behind.'

No one took that last sentence seriously, but Birch certainly took the first sentences seriously.

Birch started to explain that there was no robbery. Asa broke in, 'Mister Marshal, I rode the train an' that's all I did.'

Colton fixed the younger Tucker with a bleak stare. 'But you stopped it, boy.'

Bud Lange said, 'But there wasn't no robbery. Don't that matter?'

Marshal Colton fished for a blue bandanna to wipe off sweat and re-pocketed the bandanna before replying. He had used that moment for thinking; it was a good ruse, he'd used it dozens of times.

'Gents, my job is to serve warrants, take folks into custody. That's all. I got a warrant for this young buck. Maybe he can talk his way clear. I got no idea an' I don't care. You understand what I'm tellin' you? I got the warrant an' that's the lad, period.'

Bruce Evans had been listening without speaking, but now he fixed his gaze on the burly man and said, 'Come outside with me for a minute, Marshal.'

Colton, the old hand looked at Bruce and sighed, 'Not on your life, mister. It's been tried a dozen times an' you want to know somethin'; offerin' to bribe a federal marshal is against the law. I'll go outside with you, but I've seen 'em get two years hard labour for what I think you got in mind.'

Bruce reddened and did not repeat his invitation.

The roadway door was abruptly slammed open and the liveryman stared at Birch Tucker as he said, 'Your horse is gone. Stole right out of my barn when I was over gettin' fed at the eatery!'

Men reacted differently to emergencies, some with families, wives and children habitually weighed risks. Birch Tucker had no such inhibitions, his Morgan horse was as close to a family as any living thing except his brother and right now whatever the outcome of his brother's predicament might be, and over the last half-hour it was beginning to look favourable for Asa, his Morgan horse was uppermost. He took the liveryman by the arm, left the jailhouse with those behind staring, and did not release his grip until he and the liveryman were at the barn.

Down there he asked if the horse had been stalled and when the liveryman nodded, Birch went looking for tracks. He found them where his horse had been led forth, followed them out back to the alley and paused to yell for the liveryman to rig him out the toughest horse he had.

While the liveryman was busying himself inside, Birch had to guess how much of a lead the thief had and when the liveryman brought forth a tall, thoroughbred-looking bay and handed over the reins Birch swung up and began tracking without haste as the liveryman called after him. 'His name's Big Ben.' But Birch Tucker was already out of sight.

The difference between the pursued and the pursuit was that the pursuer was hindered by having to read sign which normally could not be done fast.

The horse thief left clear sign as long as he avoided the coach road, which he did for several miles. He had ridden fast for as long as he could see Battleboro over his shoulder. After that he veered on an angling course as far as the roadway. From there he rode due north.

Tracking on a travelled road was not as easy as tracking over grassland. Dozens of shod horses had left sign in both directions. Birch had shod his Morgan horse two weeks earlier so the tracks were not especially outstanding. Birch rode slowly sorting tracks. He could dispose of wagon animals and some saddle horses by the size of their feet. His Morgan horse wore shoes of moderate size, which made it possible for Birch to sift through other tracks until he was down to animals with average saddle-horse feet. There were enough of those tracks to make him stop several times until the set of marks he had been following were less difficult to read.

The horse thief was taking his time for an obvious reason; if pursuit appeared he would need an animal capable of running.

Birch's big thoroughbred had a skimpy mane, an easy disposition and if he had quirks Birch never found them.

Birch had no idea how much bottom the big thoroughbred had but he knew how much his Morgan horse had; it would take an exceptionally tough animal to keep up with his Morgan.

The sun was reddening off in the west; there were shadowed uplands ahead. The tracks he followed didn't deviate. The horse thief was heading north.

As long as daylight continued, Birch worried less than he would worry after dusk arrived when tracks in layers of roadway dust would play hell with visibility.

Abruptly, and for no apparent reason, the horse thief left the stage road about two miles from the place where he and his partner had shot Birch.

Except for failing light tracking over open country would be easier. Big Ben seemed to favour softer ground. Even for a tall horse he had a long stride.

The tracks hugged the lower flat country with the timbered higher country to the north. Birch came across a game trail, the kind deer made between timbered uplands and grassland. The horse thief rode that trail until it began to angle northward, then he stopped long enough to leave a brown paper cigarette butt behind, then struck out up the game trail.

It would be impossible to read sign

in the timber with daylight fading but Big Ben travelled the uphill incline with the same ability he covered flat country which put Birch well along on the crooked deer trail until he had to dismount and lead the tall horse to be closer to the ground and even then he had to pause often to see tracks.

They startled some kind of a big bird. It sprang into the air with a startled squawk and Birch tightened his grip on the reins but Big Ben neither balked nor humped up.

They reached a little clearing, this time startling two cow elks out of their beds.

The tracks disappeared in the clearing. Birch had to bend over to follow bent grass and weeds.

He could have halted; his prey probably was feeling safe by now, but he kept going, almost at a crawl in most places until the tracks became totally indiscernible.

Birch had no coat. When the chill arrived he stayed close to the bay horse, any warmth was better than none.

He went to gather twigs for a fire. As he was dumping an armload the tall horse threw up its head, little ears stiffly pointing. The grass he'd cropped protruded from both sides of his mouth. He neither chewed nor moved.

Birch yanked the tie-down loose and slowly turned expecting either a big cat or a bear. He was peering north-easterly when he picked up the faint scent of smoke.

He abandoned the notion of making a fire, led Big Ben and prowled in the direction of smoke. It was dark, huge over-ripe fir trees made movement difficult without a lot of zigzagging. He kept the smoke scent in his face. Underfoot were centuries of shed fir needles, spongy to walk over.

A horse nickered and Birch's heart lurched. He'd heard that call a hundred times.

Big Ben hung back a step or two and raised his head. Birch clamped hard down on his nostrils.

The nickering sound was not repeated. Whoever was with the horse had undoubtedly done as Birch had done, stopped the nickering horse from repeating his nicker, which was not loud, nickering horses were never loud. The reason was elemental, horses trumpeted a loud noise, they only nickered softly when they had picked up the close-by scent of another horse.

Birch sought a low branch, looped the reins and went ahead with smoke-scent strong until he could make out a small fire in an equally small clearing.

His Morgan horse was standing like a statue. By now it had also picked up man-scent. The horse hadn't been abused; where he stood, wild timothy reached almost to his knees. The horse thief was evidently an individual who cared for animals.

Birch paused beside a massive old tree, placed his left hand against rough bark for balance as he leaned to peer around. The fire was burning down, was making more smoke as it died.

He was straightening back when a man said, 'Move, mister, an' I'll kill you.'

Birch froze.

Five or six seconds later the same voice said, 'Shuck the pistol.'

Birch obeyed, moving slowly and carefully.

The next time the man spoke he said, 'Who are you . . . gawddammit, I know you.'

Birch spoke softly. 'You'd ought to, you're the other one, the feller with the redhead when he shot me.' He hung fire briefly before asking a question. 'How'd you get this far from Barnum?'

'They set me loose. I borrowed a horse over there.'

'Why did you come over here?'

'You ask a lot of questions for a feller that's got one foot in the grave an' t'other one on a banana peel. You see that bay horse over yonder, the husky feller with the wavy mane an' tail? If we hadn't been broke I wouldn't have agreed for Red to sell him.

'His name's Jesse. I broke him at three. We been partners a long time.' Bonner Watkins hesitated before speaking again. 'There's no bounty on me, if that's why you come up here.'

'Mister, I don't give a good gawddamn about you. I want my horse back.'

'Set down, don't do nothin' cute. Just set down . . . You got a hideout?'

'Never carried one, Mr Watkins.'

'*Set!*'

Birch sat. The unkempt horse thief walked around until they faced each other, one standing the other sitting. Watkins let his right hand hang. 'You're the law from Battleboro?'

'Until they can find someone.'

'How's your head?'

'Well enough. That partner of yours . . . he was close, he should have done better.'

'He thought he did. So did I. There was blood enough.' Watkins hunkered on his heels. 'I need your money, then you can start walkin' back.'

Birch emptied his pocket for green-backs. The men looked steadily at one another for a moment or two before Bonner Watkins said, 'You're a 'breed In'ian?'

'Yes. That was my brother they jailed for murder over at — '

'You're darker'n him.'

Birch shrugged. 'Always have been. He's still my brother . . . You goin' to talk me to death, Mr Watkins?'

'No, I'm tryin' to figure what to do with you.'

'Take the money, I'll take my horse an' that'll end it.'

Bonner Watkins pulled a sardonic small smile. 'I risked my hide to get over where the Morgan was an' to steal him. I need that horse, mister. You got a name?'

'Birch Tucker. Asa Tucker's my brother, younger'n me and lighter. I keep the horse, Mr Watkins.'

'Not if I shoot you.'

'That's what it'll take. You been up in this area before?'

'No, an' by tomorrow it won't matter.'

'There's a minin' camp about a mile from here up through the timber on a sidehill. A gunshot'll carry that far.'

'I didn't see no sign, no road nor trail.'

'You would have if it'd been daylight an' you'd made camp a half-mile or so up yonder.'

Bonner Watkins shifted position and leathered his six-gun. 'You got some chewin', lawman?'

Birch didn't chew, he smoked. He tossed a half-full sack of Bull Durham to the horse thief who eyed it dispassionately. Smoking tobacco made damned poor eating tobacco. He went to work building a cigarette occasionally looking over at his prisoner. He lit up with a faggot from the dying fire, exhaled and seemed to loosen as he spoke again.

'I'll leave you trussed to a tree, come mornin' you can yell'n maybe them miners'll find you. How good is that big thoroughbred-lookin' horse?'

'Sound as new money, no bad habits I could find. I got him from the liveryman in town. You leave the Morgan an' take him.'

Bonner Watkins made that disagreeable little smile again. 'Mister, you don't tell me what to do. No one ever does again. I got enough of that from Red. I'll take both horses an' you walk. That's better'n gettin' shot, ain't it?'

'Mr Watkins, I didn't come up here to let you ride off on my horse.'

The humourless smile lingered. 'Nothin' you can do about it, lawman.'

Since the horse thief had holstered his Colt, Birch had been speculating about the distance between them, which wasn't too great, but the fire ring with its red-hot coals would play hell if Birch's springing jump fell short.

Big Ben nickered. The Morgan horse answered and started walking. He liked company.

Birch said, 'Throw somethin'. That big bay horse'll fight a buzz saw.'

Bonner Watkins twisted to watch Jesse approach the tethered tall horse and Birch took down one fast deep breath and launched himself.

Watkins jerked around. His right hand dropped but the darker man hit him hard. They both went to the ground. Birch felt along the arm to the right hand and locked fingers around it eight inches from the holstered pistol.

Bonner Watkins wrenched and twisted, grunted and flung both arms. Birch ducked and turned. One knotty fist caught him in the chest. He reared back and swung. When the blow landed it sounded like a very distant pistol shot. He had to strike twice more before Bonner Watkins wilted.

Birch flung the horse-thief's gun away, stood up, brushed off as he turned to watch the horses. Neither of them was a fighter. His Morgan horse had always liked company. Evidently so did Big Ben; after smelling each other they stood side by side.

Birch went over the unconscious

horse thief for hideout weapons, tied Watkins to a gnarled tree in a hugging posture and went to saddle Jesse, get astride and strike out southward leading the taller horse.

Eventually Bonner Watkins would recover. It would take time to gnaw through the rope after which he could pick up the greenbacks, his gun and go in search of the mining camp where he could steal another animal.

The reason he wouldn't be successful was because there was no mining camp. If he persisted in travelling northward he'd have a lot of rough upland country to cross before he saw a ranch or a village.

By the time Birch got back to Battleboro it was close to dawn, sickly grey and colder than a witch's bosom.

He left the horses in the runway and went to the harness room to roust out the liveryman. It took a little rousting, the older man was sound asleep under some salt-stiff saddle blankets that smelled powerfully of old horse sweat.

When Birch used the handle of a buggy whip on the soles of the sleeping man's feet he awakened, sat up and rubbed his eyes. Birch said, 'How much do you want for the big bay horse?'

The liveryman stopped rubbing. 'Forty dollars. I been tryin' to sleep for Chris'sake.'

'Thirty dollars.'

'Birch, he's thoroughbred. That's what I gave for him.'

'Thirty dollars.'

'I worked like a' coon today, I'm dog-ass tired. Forty dollars and you get the halter.'

Birch rummaged his pocket before remembering he had no money. 'Thirty-five dollars.'

The older man yawned. 'Done. Now leave me be.'

'I got no money with me. I'll bring it to town in a day or two. Is that all right?'

'Yes, that's all right. Now I'd like to — '

'Where's my brother?'

'I got no idea.'

'He didn't go with them federal marshals?'

'No. That tough-talkin' heavyset lawman got drunk at Rory's place. His partner took on a load too. Last I saw of any of 'em they was sort of holdin' to one another following that sheriff from Barnum, on their way back where they come from. That marshal won't be back. Rory took the warrant for your brother out'n his coat and burnt it in the stove. How'll that sound when he gets back up to Denver?' The older man squirmed back under the saddle blankets and said, 'Come to town tomorrow. Rory an' Bruce Evans can tell you better'n I can. Gawddammit, good night.'

Birch was tired, whiskey-stubbled, dirty and had aches where he hadn't known a man could get them as he mounted the Morgan horse, led the tall thoroughbred and rode westerly in the direction of home.

He would return but not for three days and when he did return he smelled of liniment.

THE END

Other titles in the
Linford Western Library:

RENEGADE BLOOD

Johnny Mack Bride

Joe Gage was a drifter who'd never had a regular job until, in Dearman, Colorado, he found steady work and met a pretty girl. But he also fell foul of the feared Hunsen clan, a family of mad, murderous renegades who decided he was their enemy. Joe had two choices: give up his future and ride out of the territory, or fight against the 'Family from Hell'. He made his decision, but he was just one man against many.